# Bumps
# ALONG THE
# way

a novel

## TAYLOR DANAE COLBERT

To my soul sisters. For every tear you've dried, every story you've told, and every laugh we've had.

And to you, Gram. For believing in every dream I ever had. Love you forever.

Summer, Second Trimester

# ONE
*Della*

Della's eyes sprung open as she lay there in the dark. She tried to keep herself calm. She began to feel her insides aching, in a good way, for just a taste. He had given it to her the night before, too, but it just wasn't enough. There was no quenching this thirst she had; she was ravenous.

She actually felt her mouth start to water as she thought about the night before. She shook her head. She didn't *need* it again. Nope, she didn't even *want* it. It was just her brain playing cruel tricks on her body.

She rolled to the side of the bed and grabbed her glass of water off the nightstand. She took one small sip, then another, then began gulping it down as though she had just traversed a desert. She waited, hoping the water had washed away the fire burning inside her. She lay back down. Covers on. Covers off. She turned to the left, then the right.

It was no use. She couldn't contain this animalistic desire any longer.

She didn't care that it had only been a day. Something inside of her was pulling on her heart, and it was strong. She rolled over to his side of the bed.

"Jackson," she whispered into his ear and she trailed her fingers up and down his bare spine. "Jack, honey, wake up."

He stirred gently, blinked twice, then popped up. He had been so much more on edge, lately, especially when it came to her.

"What? What is it, hon? You okay?" he asked.

"Shh," she said, covering her hand with his. She paused, looking into his beautiful brown eyes. She took him in, every inch of his perfectly-cut face, his lips, his nose. She loved this man more than anything. And she knew he wanted to give her what she wanted as badly as she wanted it. She took a breath.

"I need cheese fries," she said.

She watched as his shoulders sunk in a combination of relief and annoyance.

"This is the third time this week," he said, rubbing his sleepy eyes with the back of his hand. "Are you sure that's good for you?"

"Hey," she said, rolling back against the headboard, "this is the first thing I've really *wanted* to eat in weeks. And since I'm not throwing up anymore, I'll eat whatever this little monster wants." She put both hands on either side of her bump, rubbing it softly. He smiled and shook his head, then leaned over to kiss her belly. "I'm so hungry right now, it's actually making me nauseous."

"One order of cheese fries, coming up," he whispered before kissing her. "It *has* to be a boy. He's clearly got my appetite." She giggled.

"No, it's definitely a girl. This little mama can

eat, too. She got it from her mama," she said.

She watched as he stood up, his blue-checkered boxers sticking closely to his butt thanks to the static electricity their enormous comforter spread to their clothes each night. He sleepily trudged over to the closet, slid on his slippers, and pulled a sweatshirt over his head. As he put his hand to the door, she stopped him.

"Um, honey? You might want to wear pants," she said. He trudged back to the closet, yanking on a pair of ratty old sweatpants. Even in the ensemble of a rodeo clown who got dressed in the dark, Jackson was a stunner. He was tall and dark, and *so* damn handsome. He was one of those guys who could pull off baggy sweatpants, or a clean-cut, perfectly tailored suit and look drop-dead gorgeous in anything. He was no longer in college basketball shape, but his naturally fit physique was one that Della had both cursed and drooled over, simultaneously. And he was just as beautiful on the inside, as corny as it sounded. She really had hit the jackpot with him.

"Okay, sweetie, I'll be back in a few," he said, leaning over to kiss her forehead one more time before heading out the door.

"I love you, baby daddy," she said, pulling the covers up to her chin. He was a cheese-fry angel.

And through her horrendous first trimester, he had been an absolute stud. He cleaned up her puke more times than she cared to admit, and had quickly learned which foods not to bring within a thirty-foot radius of her nose. He made dinner every night during the first few weeks when she was so exhausted she could barely move. Pregnancy had hit her hard.

And when their friends had made comments, and applauded him about how much he was doing, he'd wave them off.

"She's literally growing a *human*," he'd say, "I think I can make a damn meal or two."

He was so utterly perfect, it hurt. That wasn't to say they didn't have their fair share of disagreements. When they were teenagers, they had bickered over Jackson's first girlfriend and her passive aggressive comments, and battled over Della wearing Jackson's best friend's letterman jacket during a pep rally. As they aged, the arguments evolved, centering around the endless stream of bills and which neighborhood they should settle down in. But at the end of every day, they still laid together, his arm draped around her body as he inhaled her hair, her shimmying up to his familiar warmth.

God, she loved him. He was her everything, and she knew that soon, he'd be this baby's everything, too. She had to admit, it pained her ever so lightly that she would no longer be the center of his universe, but she also loved the thought of him being so in love with their child that she swore her heart was going to explode.

One of her best memories with Jackson wasn't even real, but a dream. It was after their second date, during their senior year of high school, the first night he had kissed her. And she remembered falling asleep in his Dalesville High basketball sweatshirt. And then she had the most amazing dream, which she still remembered explicitly years later.

In it, they were a few years older, on a beach, probably Ocean City, where her family had a condo. Della sat stretched out in a beach chair soaking in the rays. She watched the beautiful little girl in front of her, maybe two or three years' old, scooping wet sand out of a blue bucket and dumping it onto a pile on the shore.

Such a beautiful, sweet, baby girl, with light brown skin, a few shades lighter than her daddy's, and a few shades darker than her mommy's. She had perfect, dark chocolate ringlets that bounced off her shoulders as she moved around in the sand. And then, suddenly, the little mocha angel popped up from her position, and began jumping up and down ecstatically.

"Daddy!" she screamed, over and over, as she ran across the sand, past Della, jumping into Jackson's arms, and Della watched as he reached the crest of a dune a few yards away from him, glowing like some sort of god. He caught the little girl as if she were a feather, smothering her in kisses and tickling her until she belly laughed. Then, he looked over to Della, wearing the smile that made her knees shaky every damn time.

And that was it. That was the extent of the dream. But damn, it was such a good one. And now, here she was, currently making it a reality as she lay in their bed.

She rolled over, grabbing her phone and scrolling through Pinterest a few times. She had chosen a bed set for a girl, a violet comforter with pink and blue flowers, but just could *not* decide on a nursery theme for a boy. As another episode of *Friends* started, she realized that he had been gone for almost a half-hour. Weird, because Andy's was only seven minutes from their house, right on Main Street in the center of Dalesville. She had timed it the last time she had made him go for a cheese-fry emergency run.

She clicked out of Pinterest and dialed him. A few rings, then his voicemail, the same message that had been in place since he graduated from high school.

*Hi there, you've reached Jackson Niles. I'm unavailable at the moment, but please leave a message and I'll call you back. Thanks!*

She hung up and flipped through the channels, trying to ease her irrational mind. There was probably a wait. Although, it was 11:43 p.m., and Andy's was one

5

of the only places that stayed open late after the rest of the town shut down. But it was still quiet, sleepy old Dalesville. The only people who would be at a bar on a Monday night in Dalesville were the same people who'd been there every night for the last forty-or-so years. There wouldn't be enough of a crowd to make Jackson late.

Trying to distract herself, Della opened Facebook on her phone, scrolling through pictures of her aunt's new cat, and her high school science teacher's kid graduating from middle school. Man, she was getting old. She stopped when she saw a picture of Luciana, arms crossed, wearing a sleek black blazer, her dark brown curls pulled back ever so professionally. The headline read: MARYLAND NATIVE MAKING WAVES IN SEATTLE. Della felt her heart swelling with enormous pride. Luci was such a *boss.* Della quickly clicked "share," adding the caption "CHECK OUT MY BEST FRIEND!" before posting. She couldn't wait to hear all about it tomorrow. She clicked out of Facebook and looked at the time again. 11:52 p.m. She texted him.

*Where are you babe? Getting worried.*

Nothing.

She called again.

*Hi there, you've reached Jackson Niles. I'm unavailable at the moment, but please leave a message and I'll call you back. Thanks!*

Okay, now she was a little panicky. She hopped out of bed and slipped on her own slippers, wrapping her robe around her bump tightly. She made her way downstairs and grabbed the keys to her Camry, and headed out in the direction of Andy's. She knew she was being overdramatic, and letting her anxiety get the best of her. He was probably almost home. He turned his ringer off all the time, and always forgot to turn it back on. She'd been getting on him for him lately, telling him he needed to break the habit before she was close to her due date.

As she drove down Route 124, the bright blue and red lights of a cop car whizzed by her on the left side. Then another. Then another. And that's when her heart began pounding in her chest.

She turned onto Main Street, and she heard the blaring sirens so loud, she actually stopped and covered her ears. Ahead, there was a flood of purple, as all the police cars sat in a heap, their lights blinking so out of sync, it made her dizzy.

Or maybe it was the fact that they were surrounding Jackson's body, lying in the middle of Main Street, blood trickling out of him and onto the pavement.

That might have had something to do with the sudden vertigo.

Nearby, another mass of officers was gathered around a young woman, maybe twenty or so. She was wrapped in a thick blanket, and she was crying hysterically as one of the female officers wrapped her arms around her.

When Della finally caught her breath, she stepped out of her car, slowly at first. She took a few, slow, drawn out steps toward the mass of cars, then her feet picked up, faster, pulling her closer.

"Sorry, ma'am, no one past this line, please," one of the officers said, sticking his arm out to block her path.

"Tommy, that's his wife," she heard another officer say. She turned her head to see Dayton Briggs, and for a moment, she forgot where she was. She hadn't seen him for years. But right now, she was actually relieved to see a familiar face, a face that might be able to tell her what the hell was going on. Someone that might be able to bring her to her Jackson. Someone to tell her everything was fine, it was just a scratch, what she was seeing wasn't real.

"Dayton?"

"Della," he said, waving to the other officer to let her through to him. As she walked, she kept one hand on her belly, as if she was shielding the baby from the horrific view.

"Dayton, please, what happened? Is he moving?"

"Della, do you want to sit—"

"*Dayton,*" she said, her eyes tearing into his, "please."

Dayton sighed and looked down at the ground before looking back up at her.

"Okay, Della, okay." Dayton put his hands on Della's shoulders, and she could feel that they were shaking. "Jackson was walking out of Andy's when he noticed a man up ahead, dragging a young woman through the parking lot. He was trying to force her into his vehicle when Jackson approached him.

"There was some sort of physical altercation, and just as Jackson threatened to call the police, the perp shot him in the chest. He knocked the woman unconscious, but she was able to come to and call 911."

Oh, God, Della felt sick. She put one hand to her mouth, the other to her belly. He paused for a moment, making sure that she was stable, before he continued.

"I was the first officer on the scene," he said, his eyes falling to the ground again. "I started compressions until the paramedics arrived, but there was no pulse. . ."

His eyes found hers, but she wasn't seeing him. She wasn't seeing anything.

"Where is he? I need to see him, please," she begged him.

"I'm so sorry, Della," Dayton said, "but Jackson is unresponsive. They've been administering CPR for almost twenty minutes now. They will take him to the hospital to see if there's anything else they can do, but he will likely be . . .dead on arrival."

She felt woozy, disoriented, like a character in a movie who was just  unrealistically close to an explosion. She felt like she was falling.

Wait, no, she actually *was* falling.

Dayton caught her, his strong arms lowering her back against one of the police cars for balance.

"Della? Della, can you hear me?"

She could, but she couldn't answer him. Behind him in the distance, she watched as an EMT did one, two, three compressions on Jackson's chest. She could still see the blood carving its way down the pavement like some sort of snake. She watched as his limbs bobbed up and down with the movements.

Then she saw another paramedic reach over and stop the EMT, pointing to his watch. The EMT climbed off of his chest, shaking his head. Then, he pulled a sheet up over Della's dead husband's face.

She clutched her belly, and let out a blood-curdling scream, that turned into a sob. She lunged in Jackson's direction.

If she could just reach him, just touch him, she knew he'd open his eyes. For her. For their baby.

But she felt Dayton's arms around her, pulling her into him, turning her away. And she let her face crash into his chest, tears soaking into his uniform.

◊

Somehow, she ended up at the hospital.

She sort of remembered Dayton asking her for her in-laws' phone number. She kind of remembered her conversation with her brother, Cash.

Then, a doctor came out from the hallway and walked toward her.

"Mrs. Niles?" she asked. Della looked up, totally lost. "I'm Dr. Clouse. I've been administering CPR on your husband for some time now. The paramedics did CPR on the scene, and our staff has been working to see if there's anything else that can be done. I'm so sorry to bring you this news, but your husband has passed away. Would you like to come say goodbye?"

Della blinked feverishly, listening, soaking in the question. No. She wouldn't like to say goodbye. Dayton reached for her hand.

"Do you want me to come with you, Della?" he asked. She shook her head, pushing herself up from the flimsy, uncomfortable waiting room chair.

She followed Dr. Clouse down a long, white, freezing-cold hallway. It felt endless. And then they reached a big, blue door. Dr. Clouse took a breath, then opened it, holding it for Della. A long curtain hung in the middle of the room.

"Now, please remember that he's a bit scratched from where he hit the pavement, and bruised from the chest compressions. Again, I'm so sorry to have to bring you this news," Dr. Clouse said. Then, she reached up and pulled the curtain back. Della stepped forward, staring down at the love of her life.

His skin had a strange purplish-greyish tint to it, and she couldn't believe how fast death had set in.

Strangely, lying there lifeless, he was still as handsome as ever. His perfect lips were pursed ever so slightly, his eyes closed. He looked calm, peaceful.

The tears burned as they ran down her cheeks. She stepped toward him, her whole body shaking, and reached for his hand.

"I'll give you a few minutes," Dr. Clouse said, rolling a stool up for Della to sit on.

Della held her hand to her mouth to stifle her sobs for a few moments. Then she pulled herself together.

"Jackson Niles," she finally said, as she held his hand to her cheek, "I can't believe this is it. I. . . I can't. . ." she paused, giving herself a moment to get it together. "I can't believe that you went out for fries and never came back." God dammit. She'd hate herself forever for waking him up. She sniffed, wiping her nose on her sleeve. "I have no idea how I'm going to do this life without you. But I will be the best mom I can be to this little munchkin, knowing we have you watching over us."

She wasn't sure how she was formulating the words she was saying. It felt like she was listening to someone else talk.

"But Jackson, you made me who I am. I will love you forever."

She kissed his hand, his cheek, his lips, letting her forehead rest against his. She sat frozen like that for a few minutes, soaking in the last time she'd ever feel his body against hers, even if he didn't have any life left in his. Then she said a last goodbye to her husband, and walked out of the room.

As she sat back in the waiting room, Dayton knelt down in front of her.

"Your in-laws are on their way up," he whispered, covering her hand with his. She nodded. They lived eight hours away in South Carolina. It would be a while.

"What about the man?" she asked. "The man who shot him? Did you find him?" Dayton hung his head.

"Not yet. He took off. The woman who called it in, she's at the station now giving a detailed description and working with a sketch artist. She told us he drove a red truck, and she's offered to be as much help as she can be. We're doing all we can. I'm sorry I don't have anything more for you on that. But I will, Della. I swear to you, I will," Dayton said.

She nodded. She knew that when she wasn't so numb, she'd feel a *whole* lot of hate for Mr. Red Truck.

"Is there anyone else I can call for you?" Dayton asked her. She stared ahead so that it seemed she was looking directly at him. But really, she wasn't seeing anything at all.

"Call Luciana. Please."

# TWO
## *Luci*

She replayed Mia's words over and over in her head. That's what Luci did. She agonized. She obsessed.

*You interviewed well, today, Luciana. We should know something soon.*

When Luci had decided to apply for the Vice President of Sales position, she was under the impression that she was the only internal candidate. Mia had made it seem like she was such a shoe-in, such a definite, the obvious choice. So what was all this "we should know something soon" business? Ugh. She hated the vagueness and politics of the corporate world, and yet, she thrived on it.

She increased the speed on her treadmill, pounding her feet with every step. It was after eleven o'clock, but she couldn't sleep. If she got this position, she'd be the youngest female in a Vice President position in all of Seattle. Probably all of Washington. And she'd be one of the first Latina women in a position like this *ever*. She could see herself on the cover of

*Forbes,* a picture similar to the one in the feature that the *Seattle Daily* had done on her, only, much better quality. She could practically see the headlines: DAUGHTER OF IMMIGRANT TACKLES SECURITY INDUSTRY. God, her parents would freak.

Her phone buzzed in the cup holder of the treadmill, snapping her back to reality. She hit the stop button as she caught her breath. She didn't recognize the number, but she did recognize the area code. It was someone from back home.

"Hello?" she asked, trying not to sound as out-of-breath as she was feeling.

"Luci?"

She sucked in a breath of air and forgot to let it out. She hadn't heard that voice saying her name in four years.

The last words he had said were burned into her mind: "I'm sorry, Luci. You deserve so much more, and I'll be praying every day that you get it." Actually, he hadn't even *said* them. He'd written them, in a stupid, unbelievably vague letter that he'd left in her mom's mailbox. And that was it. No calls, no texts, no answers to hers. Not exactly the proper way to end a five-year-relationship.

Some days, it felt like an eternity ago, like an entirely different lifetime. And some nights, when she lay alone in her studio apartment in downtown Seattle, it felt like the breakup had been that very morning.

"Hello? Luciana?" he asked again. She swallowed hard.

"Why are you calling me?" she finally asked, after seriously contemplating hitting the end button.

"It's Della. She asked me to call you," he said quickly, almost as if he knew she might hang up any second.

"Della? What happened? Is she okay? Is it the

baby?"

"No, no, Della is fine. It's Jackson. He was. . .he was shot tonight, and, well. . . he didn't. . . he didn't make it. They officially pronounced him dead just a few minutes ago at the hospital."

Luci covered her mouth and sunk to the floor, her weight falling limp onto the wall next to the treadmill.

"Wha-what? Are you sure? *Shot?*"

"Yes. I know, it's sort of unbelievable that something like this could happen in our little town. But I was the first officer on the scene. I'm so sorry, Luci—"

"Where is Della now? Who is with her?"

"Her in-laws are on their way up from South Carolina, and I think she said her brother is driving up from Morgan State, too. But right now, it's just me."

"I'm getting on the next flight. Please don't leave her until someone is there."

"I will stay right here," he said. "I can pick you up from the airport, if you need," he added after a pause. "Her brother should be here in the next half-hour or so."

"No, thank you. I'll take a cab." She fumbled around to hit "end," her hands trembling.

Oh, Jesus, Jackson.

This couldn't be happening. Not to her Jackson. Not to her Della. Della and Jackson, they had been, well, Della and Jackson, for so long now. They were a unit. And even though he was the one who ultimately "stole" her best friend, Luci knew they were supposed to be together. Della and Jackson were what every other couple should strive for, in Luci's opinion. They moved so effortlessly together, yet, they never abandoned who they were as individuals. And Luci had sobbed like a baby on their wedding day, barely able to get through her speech.

Over the last few years, Luci had really started to consider Jackson to be one of her best friends, too. They had the same sense of humor, they were both die-hard Capitals fans, and most importantly, she knew Jackson's love for Della was as deep, sincere and unconditional as Luci's own love for her best friend.

And when they FaceTimed Luci the night they got their positive pregnancy test, her heart grew three sizes. A baby was all Della had ever wanted, and Luci couldn't thank Jackson enough for making her best friend so damn happy.

But now he was lying in a morgue somewhere with a hole in his chest.

Luci shuddered as she threw only the essentials into one of her Chanel suitcases, closing it without surveying what she had packed like she normally would. She knew when she landed, she'd likely need to go shopping, or borrow some of Della's clothes. But that was the least of her worries.

She moved like a zombie through the airport security, not even flinching when the TSA agents hollered at her to take off her shoes for the second time. Time was moving so slow, yet, she knew on the other side of the country, for her best friend, time had moved too damn fast. And now, she'd never get time she wanted most, her time with Jackson, back again.

◊

Luci somehow managed to sleep for most of the flight, despite the minor turbulence just before they landed.

She was normally so happy to see the "Welcome to Baltimore" mural that hung from ceiling at baggage claim. But right now, it seemed to be mocking her. *Welcome home, have fun mourning your friend's dead husband while we eat crabs and drink some Natty Boh*, it seemed to say, taunting her.

But when her cab finally pulled into Dalesville, she had a moment of peace. The sun was just now rising over the farm as they drove past, peeking over the lines of black trees in the distance. A thin layer of fog stretched out in random blotches across the grass and road. It felt good to be back in Maryland.

But then, as the cab pulled up in front of Jackson and Della's little bungalow, she felt her heart shattering into a tiny, million pieces. She paid her fare and got out, dragging her bag across the driveway and up the four cement porch steps. Before she could knock, the door opened. There stood Cash, Della's younger brother, staring back at her. Luci dropped her bag and wrapped her arms around him, holding onto him tight.

"How is she?" she whispered.

"Exhausted," Cash said, kneeling down to pick up her suitcase. "She's so tired. And so, so sad. His parents should be here soon, but I think they are going to a hotel," Cash said, rubbing his swollen eyes. "I can't believe he's dead."

Jackson had been more of a brother than a brother-in-law to Cash, one of his very best friends.

"Is any of your family coming?" Luci asked. Cash nodded.

"Aunt Bea is coming in tomorrow afternoon with Grams. Should be interesting," he said with a half-smile. It was a well-known fact that the Mears family was a bit of a handful. And ever since Mr. and Mrs. Mears had died, Della's Aunt Bea had been a bit overbearing, to put it politely. It didn't take long after Della and Jackson moved into their own place for Cash to move in with them, getting rid of any need for Aunt Bea. She was their father's oldest sister, and a bossy one at that.

"Hopefully we can get her out of here sooner rather than later," Cash said with a smile.

"How are you holding up?" Luci asked, throwing her arm back around his shoulders. This was a lot of weight for Cash to carry.

"I'm okay. I wish mom was alive. Or even dad, although, he wouldn't really know what to say. I just don't really know how to help her," Cash said, his voice cracking into almost a whimper. "And honestly, I'm struggling, too."

Luci nodded and pulled him in for another hug.

Two years ago, right after Jackson and Della's wedding, Mrs. Mears had been diagnosed with stage four breast cancer. She was given a six-month prognosis, but lasted two. Six months later, the police found Mr. Mears' car crashed into a creek a few towns over. He'd picked up a bottle the day Mrs. Mears died, and never put it down. Cash was all Della had left, and he took the role seriously.

"You're doing great, Cash. She's so lucky to have you. Now, let me go see this girl of mine. Why don't you try and get some sleep?" Cash nodded.

"I'm so glad you're here, Luci. She needs you," he said, slowly trudging up to the guest bedroom.

Luci took a deep breath before making her way up the stairs, and gently turning the knob to Jackson and Della's bedroom.

Through the stream of hall light, she could see Della's silhouette, curled up in the fetal position on what Luci knew was Jackson's side of the bed. She tiptoed across the floor, slipping off her shoes, and gently laying down so she was facing Della nose-to-nose. Her beautiful, exhausted Della. Her heartbroken Della, who would probably never be the same. Della's eyes opened slowly, blinking a few times as she squinted. She closed them again, letting out a long sigh, one of relief.

"You're here," she whispered. Then the sobs came. Luci scooted in closer, pulling Della into her. "He's gone, Luci. He's gone. My Jackson. Oh, God, my Jackson."

"Shhh," Luci whispered, stroking Della's long, straight, strawberry-blonde hair.

What the fuck was she supposed to say now?

When no genius response came to mind, Luci just pulled her friend in to her even closer.

"Shhh," she whispered again.

"Luci?"

"Yes, Dell?"

"Will you come with me to the funeral home?" she asked. "Oh God, I have to plan my husband's funeral," she added, as if she were just now coming to the realization herself. Luci swallowed hard.

"Of course."

# THREE
*Della*

Della's eyes opened slowly, and with every ounce of light she let in, came another image from the night before that had seared itself into her memory. She pictured Jackson's blood pouring from his body into the street, his hands and feet gently popping up and down as his chest heaved, his face expressionless in the colored lights of the police cars. She stared at the ceiling as she realized that that image of him lying there, lifeless on the pavement, would stick with her forever.

She looked over at the alarm clock on her nightstand, the one with the fraying cord that Jackson had told her to replace months ago. 11:22 a.m. Holy shit. She couldn't remember the last time she had slept this long. She had quit her teaching job when they found out she was pregnant, and Jackson got his promotion, but even still, the morning sickness had her up at all hours.

She rolled over slowly, hand on her belly, to face Luci, who was sound asleep. She looked tired, and Della knew the traveling had to have been a lot. But she was so happy Luci was with her. In her bed. On Della's side, because Della was on Jackson's side.

Jackson. Her dead husband. Her husband who just ran out to get her an order of cheese fries. Her stupid, stupid late-night request that she would kick herself for until the end of time.

Her husband, Jackson. Who was dead.

She sat up slowly, letting reality wash over her fully.

"Hi, Della Bee," Luci said, sitting up and rubbing her eyes.

"Morning," Della said, sliding off the bed.

She made her way to the bathroom, one hand on her belly, and one hand on her back. She'd had annoying back pain ever since the start of her second trimester. It wasn't terrible, but just enough to make things like getting out of bed, or getting up from the recliner in the living room, a hell of a task.

"You look adorable," Luci said, smiling. "I just realized that this is the first time I've actually seen you pregnant in person. I love it."

A small smirk spread across Della's face, then floated away just as quickly as it had appeared. There was one thing on her mind, and it seemed to be blocking everything else out.

"Well," Della said, reappearing after only a minute or two in the bathroom, "let's get this over with."

"Are you sure you want to go today? It's so soon," Luci protested. But Della just shook her head.

"No, it needs to be today. I need to make sure they can do it next week, and I want to get to the cemetery to make sure I can get two plots," Della said so matter-of-factly, that she actually surprised herself. She was walking and talking like she just had some mundane, routine errands to run—not like she was planning the final farewell for her beloved husband. Luci threw her black curls up into a messy bun, pulled on a pair of leggings, and followed Della out the door.

The next few hours whizzed by, and Della continued to function in the same haze she'd been in since she saw Jackson's truck. She knew she took out her checkbook at both the funeral home and the cemetery, but she had no idea how much she'd written down. And she didn't really care. She knew that Jackson's life insurance would end up covering it all, and then some. She knew that she had picked out a headstone, and that she'd chosen the words "beloved father, husband, and friend," to appear beneath his name, even though he would never live to be a father. And she knew that she had chosen the perfect double-plot at the cemetery so that one day, she'd be lying there with him.

But at the end of the day, she was exhausted. She'd gone through a widow's motions, without ever stopping to realize that she was, in fact, a widow.

Luci slid down on the couch next to her, handing Della a bowl of cereal, the only thing she could stomach right now.

"Are you sure you can stay here that long?" Della asked. They had set the funeral for the following Thursday.

"Of course," Luci said. "I'm not going anywhere." Della smiled as Luci took her hand. Thank God for this beautiful, beautiful creature. She was pretty sure there was no way in hell she'd make it through the next week without her.

The rest of the week dragged on, with Luci and Cash trying desperately to get Della out of the house, but to no avail. They answered the door graciously every time someone delivered a frozen meal, and acted as Della's personal secretaries whenever her cell phone rang. She wasn't ready to talk about Jackson. She wasn't ready to go through the details of his death. She wasn't ready to get back to her life, now that she'd be living it without him.

Della woke up early on Thursday morning so she could try and give her board-straight hair some sort of volume and apply some waterproof makeup. She had searched Amazon the week before for a black, funeral-appropriate maternity dress. She slipped into her most comfortable pair of black flats; despite the fact that it was her husband's funeral, her feet were occasionally starting to swell now, and she hated trying to navigate grass in heels. Sorry, Jackson, flats would have to do.

She smiled to herself in the mirror for a quick moment; she knew if he were here, he'd smack her tush and tell her she looked smokin' hot, no matter what she was wearing, or how massive her belly had become.

When she made it downstairs, Cash and Luci were waiting for her at the kitchen table. They both stood up as if she were making some grand entrance. Luci held out her hand.

"Let's do this," she said.

The whole way to the church, Della stared blankly ahead. When they arrived, she couldn't believe how packed the place was. Every pew from front to back was loaded, and there were people she recognized from all walks of their life standing at the back of the room.

Reverend Kyle walked in, nodding at her, and asked if she was ready to begin. She scanned the room, but her in-laws were nowhere to be found. Finally, the back doors opened, and a rush of people came through, chattering loudly, as if they didn't know they were in a church. It actually made Della smile.

Truth be told, Della and Jackson were not religious. Like, at all. But with the speed of things, and how quickly she had to make decisions, she landed on the Baptist church in town that Jackson's family always went to whenever they were visiting. Which wasn't a lot. They saw his family maybe two or three times a year. She smiled at their tardiness; as long as she had known them, they were consistently late.

"The Niles family is famous for being on our own time," Jackson would tell her, "so remember to always tell them the starting time is at least a half-an-hour earlier than it actually is. And be careful. The longer you're married to me, you'll find yourself on Niles time, too."

And damn if he wasn't right. Della couldn't be on time to save her life anymore.

When her in-laws had arrived early the morning after Jackson had passed, Della was so glad to see them. Honestly, she didn't know them all that well, despite the fact that she and Jackson had been together since high school. Once Jackson graduated, his parents made their way back down to the small town in South Carolina where his father had grown up. Jackson's grandmother had grown too frail to live on her own, and they knew she could never live up north. They visited a few times a year, and they alternated between South Carolina and Maryland for Christmases.

Della waved them to the front, where she had reserved the front pew for herself, Cash, and Luci. They each hugged her, kissed her cheeks, and took their seats. Della nodded to Reverend Kyle.

"Good morning, everyone, and thank you all for being here today," he said. She felt her mother-in-law squeeze her hand as she wept quietly, her father-in-law with his arm around her shoulder.

"I love you, Elyse," Della whispered in her ear.

Elyse pulled Della's head in close.

"I love you, too, baby," she whispered. "And me and Tony, we will always be here for you and that little one."

Della smiled at her, tears welling in her eyes, and nodded.

She turned back to Reverend Kyle. She'd smile faintly whenever he mentioned "Jackson's loving and devoted wife," but the rest of the service slogged by. She tuned out now and then just to keep from falling apart entirely. As the service came to a close, everyone rose and she followed closely, noticing for a short moment how surreal it was, walking behind her husband, who lay dead in a casket. And afterward, she hugged more people than she could count, each of whom seemed unfazed by the fact that Della was still standing, even though the reality of it shocked her.

At the cemetery, Cash and Luci each took one of her hands, helping her through the freshly mowed grounds as if she were trying out a new pair of legs. The truth was, they both knew she was clumsy as a newborn deer even on a good day, and she couldn't be trusted to stay upright without help. Not when she was carrying such precious cargo.

While Reverend Kyle waited for the rest of the attendees to get situated, Della received even more hugs—way more than she'd bargained for. As she went from one teary-eyed person to the next, she felt herself growing more and more tired. She had to put up a front, the "tough widow" front; she couldn't cry back to the crying people. Instead, she had to let them know she'd be okay. She and the baby would be fine. They'd get through this. She'd smile, patting their shoulders. Comforting *them.*

"I'm so sorry, Della."

"Is there anything I can do?"

"What do you need?"

She was getting real sick and tired of answering the same questions over, and over, and over again. Finally, Luci took her hand, rescuing her from the whirlpool of people.

Just as Reverend Kyle was getting ready to begin the burial service, Della felt a tap on her shoulder. She turned to a young woman—the same young woman from the scene the night Jackson died—standing before her. She was petite, barely over five-feet tall, with beautiful, wavy, chocolate brown hair and striking blue eyes. This was the girl. This was the girl Jackson saved. This was the girl Jackson died for, instead of coming home to his pregnant wife.

"Mrs. Niles, my name is Cora Black. I'm—" the young woman started to say, but Della cut her off.

"I know who you are. You're the woman my husband died trying to help when you were too drunk to take care of yourself."

Cora's jaw snapped shut as she took a step back, gripping onto her own arm.

"I. . . uh," Cora started to say.

"Ladies and gentlemen," Reverend Kyle began to say. Della turned away.

"Excuse me. I have to bury my husband, now," she said.

Cora stepped back, disappearing into the crowd of people gathering behind her.

 Della sat in the chair underneath the green canopy as Reverend Kyle said a few last words.

She felt her hands go numb, and her body started to shake. Luci and Cash held to her tight, keeping her steady.

Then she watched as the cemetery staff lowered Jackson's shiny oak casket lower, and lower, and lower.

And she sat still as her heart jumped out of her chest, taking its final resting place in the cold, hard ground.

# FOUR
*Luci*

Although it was June, Luci felt a shiver go down her spine as she watched the final lowering of one of her very best friends into his grave.

Good God. Jackson had a *grave*. And next to the giant hole in the ground was a small yellow marker stuck in the dirt. It was marking Della's future grave. Luci shivered again. It was too weird.

She felt Della putting more and more weight on her as she grew weaker, both from emotion, and actual exhaustion. She wouldn't dare say it out loud for fear of coming across as selfish—after all, it wasn't her husband who had died—but Luci was struggling big time with this. She hated seeing the people she loved in pain. But she also genuinely missed the crap out of Jackson. They connected on a different level, and always had. He was so good to Della, so perfect for her, that Luci wasn't sure how Della would ever find someone so perfect again. Maybe she never would.

Luci's own mother came up from behind her,

wrapping her arms around Luci and kissing her cheeks. She rubbed Della' shoulders before walking across the grass. She had offered to host the reception at her house, knowing it would be too much for Della to deal with.

"Plus," her mother had said, "If Della needs to get out early, you can take her back home where she can rest."

Luci had missed her mother so much when she was in Seattle, but she came to visit her often. Her mother was so proud of all she was doing, both in her career, and now, with her friend.

"Your father is proud of you, too," her mother had told her the day before. She smiled and nodded, finding herself wondering what her father was doing in this moment. She did miss him, but it had been so long since she'd seen him, that her heart had grown thick to protect itself.

And just as she waited for a few more crowds of people to pass, Dayton caught her eye, standing at the far corner of the canopy, staring down into the gaping hole in the ground. She felt her body tensing up, as if she needed to put up her best defense. As if he was about to walk right over to her, and yank her heart out of her chest all over again.

Ugh. Dayton. She hated that he made her swell up with anger, and retreat with sadness and longing, all at the same damn time. Damn Dayton, with his sandy brown hair trimmed perfectly and his glistening gray eyes. His hair was so shaggy when they were kids, and she used to love ruffling her fingers through it. But, as much as she hated to admit it, he looked good like this, too. She assumed he had to clean himself up a bit for the police academy. It suited him.

She still hated his freaking guts. But right now, he looked so sad that she had to fight a strong urge to run to him and throw her arms around him. Let him cry on her. Rub his head.

In high school, Jackson and Dayton had been best friends—like, Della-and-Luci level of best friends. But after their breakup, things got weird between the two boys, and Luci always felt a little bit sorry about that. She knew Della hated Dayton almost as much as she did because of what he did to Luci, which, in turn, meant Jackson would see him a lot less. They still stayed in touch, but slowly, Dayton was excluded from a lot of gatherings, even the ones where it was just the guys.

Now, she saw his eyes trail in her direction, and she quickly looked away, grabbing hold of Della's arm to start making their way to the car.

"Need a hand?" she heard Dayton's scruffy voice ask, barely a moment later.

"We got it, thanks," Luci scoffed back, brushing past him as she picked up the pace.

"Oh, wait," Della said, pausing to turn back to Dayton. "Is there any word on him? On the man?"

Dayton's eyes fell to the ground, as he shook his head slowly.

"Not yet, Della, I'm sorry. We are working on it, though, I promise." Della nodded her head slowly, turning back toward the car.

◊

Back at her mother's house, Luci was making small talk with just about everyone. Some people she was actually happy to catch up with, like Olivia, Jamie, and Bria, good friends from high school. Others, like Joanna, Dayton's only other girlfriend ever, she was less excited to see. But it was sincerely comforting to see the huge troves of people coming from near and far to support Della, and to remember Jackson. He was such a good person, and it showed in the tears of every person at the house.

Luci was pleased to help her mother host; she distracted herself from the tears and sadness by filling up sandwich trays and making punch. Once she had at least greeted everyone in the room, she excused herself, pushing the heavy swinging door in her mother's kitchen and pulling out more sandwiches from the fridge. She was placing them on the tray carefully, one by one in a circular pattern, when she heard his voice, and almost dropped the whole thing.

"Luci?" he asked. She jumped first, then rolled her eyes. She refused to turn to him. "Do you need help with anything?"

"No, I'm fine. Thanks," she said, never taking her eyes off the deli meat in front of her.

"Luci, I know this is a bad time, but do you think we could talk sometime, later today?" She scoffed and whipped her head in his direction.

"Yeah, Dayton. This is a bad time. This is a very bad time," she said, flying past him with the huge sandwich tray and out the door again. No way was she going to make time for him and his bullshit. And today, of all days. No *way*.

Luci stood in the background listening to the questions that flew around the room. Some were concerned with Della's finances; how would she manage after Jackson's life insurance ran out? Some were concerned with the baby; children need a father-figure, you know. Luci's head was spinning, so she knew Della's was, too. Luci was pretty sure that Della had no answers to these questions yet, and as much as she tried to fight it, they made Luci anxious, too. How would her Della manage this? But she also felt protective. Who were these people to question her best friend's ability to raise her own child.

Finally, as the badgering died off and the night calmed a bit, Luci could see that Della needed to leave. She wasn't even crying anymore; she was just exhausted.

"Alright, mom, are you okay if we head out?" Luci asked, pulling her purse up onto her shoulder.

"Of course, sweetie," she said. Her mother walked them to the door, kissing both of their cheeks as they made their way out.

"Thank you so much for doing this, Miss Carolyn," Della told her, her voice defeated. They'd called each other's parents "Miss First Name" and "Mister First Name" since they were in the first grade, and there was no going back now.

"Oh, you stop with all that 'thank you' nonsense," Carolyn said, giving Della another hug. "I am right around the corner, if you ever need me."

Della nodded, squeezing her right back. After Luci's father was deported back to Cuba when the girls were seven, Della's parents had taken to being there for anything and everything Mrs. Ruiz and the kids needed. They became a sort of family unit, the three parents talking on a weekly basis, keeping tabs on all of their kids together.

And when Mr. and Mrs. Mears passed, Della and Luci felt the grip of Mrs. Ruiz tighten on all of them, as if she were clutching to what she had left as the last parent standing. She had been calling Della every week to check in on the pregnancy. She'd made her and Jackson dinner a few times when Della was so sick during her first trimester. She'd been there for everything, and Luci was so thankful that her mother could be there for Della while Luci was across the country.

When they got back to Della's, Luci propped pillows up underneath her friend's feet on the couch. Cash grabbed a bag of chips from the cupboard and yanked the top off the guacamole container.

As he walked into the living room, Della sat straight up.

"What is *that?*" she asked, eyeing the guac.

"It's . . . " Luci started to say.

"Get it *out* of here! Please!" Della cried. Cash quickly snapped the container shut, running the guac out of the living room as if he were carrying a bomb.

When he came back in, Della was munching on plain tortilla chips.

"Sorry about that," she said. "Apparently I don't like guac anymore."

Luci and Cash smiled at each other and shook their heads. Luci slumped down on the couch, lifting Della's feet and placing them on her lap.

"So, you ready to go back to school, Cash?" Luci asked him. He smiled faintly.

"I guess so," he said, reaching for Della's hand. "But I don't want to leave you."

Della shot him a look.

"I am going to be okay, kiddo," she said, ruffling his hair. "I promise."

Cash smiled, sitting back against the blue chair, seemingly satisfied with that answer. After a few episodes of *George Lopez* and almost an entire bag of chips, sans guac, he kissed each of them on their foreheads and went up to bed.

Just as Luci was starting to get up herself, her phone rang.

"Be right back," she said. She opened the large sliding glass door to Della and Jackson's back patio, and stepped outside.

"Hello?"

"Hi, Luciana. It's Mia."

"Hey, Mia," she said, feeling her nerves stand on end. With everything going on, she'd quite honestly forgotten about her job for a few days. Luci wasn't like a lot of people, who looked forward to breaks from work. Her breaks were *in* her work. She loved the thrill of her job, the satisfaction of making and surpassing her expected sales numbers, the victory of snagging a new client. But Della needed her, so that's where she was.

"I hope things are going okay there. I wanted to call and let you know that the executive team reconvened today, and we'd like to extend the job offer to you. We'd like you to be our new Vice President of Sales."

In one fell swoop, Luci felt her heart rise and sink, as if it were on the scariest roller coaster in the country. She had worked so hard for this; she'd waited so patiently. She'd consistently worked sixty-hour weeks, going the extra mile, meeting with clients after hours, solidifying deals. She deserved this. She wanted this.

But in the same breath, a few feet away, sat her very best friend, all alone in this big world now.

"Wow, that is great news," Luci said, breathlessly. "Can I give you an answer tomorrow?" There was a pause on the other end.

"I have to say, Luciana, I wasn't expecting hesitation, but yes, protocol is forty-eight hours to make a decision."

"Thanks, Mia."

"Have a good night. My thoughts are with your friend."

Luci sighed, resting her head against the siding of the house before making her way back inside. She plopped back down on the couch, grabbing the bowl of chips and fishing through to find anything that wasn't just a crumb.

"Was that work?" Della asked.

"Yeah."

"Everything okay?"

"Huh? Oh, yeah. They are just anxious to get me back."

"Speaking of that, when are you going back?" Della asked. Luci raised her eyebrows. This was the million-dollar question she'd been asking herself all week.

How long was long enough to stay with your widowed, pregnant, best friend? How many days, weeks, months, should she spend taking care of her? Was there a real answer to this?

"Luci, when are you going back?" Della asked again.

Luci didn't speak; she just shrugged her shoulders. Della sat up, a crease forming on her shirt between her boobs and her bulging belly. She snatched the bowl away, putting it back on the table.

"Luciana Catalina Ruiz," she said, and Luci shot her a look. "You are going back to Seattle. This week. Aren't you supposed to have that big interview soon, anyway? You can't stay here with me forever. You have to go back. I will be fine."

Della took her hands, and Luci immediately felt guilty. She should be giving Della a pep-talk, giving her comfort. Not the other way around.

"Are you sure?" Luci managed to ask. And Della smiled, nodded, and pulled her in for a hug.

"Luce, you have a life. You have to get back to it. I love you for worrying about me, but I love you *too* much for you to put anything at stake," she said.

Luci gave her a sad smile.

"I love you, too," she said.

After a few more minutes, Luci pulled out her

laptop, checking airfares and flight times. She looked at Della, who was drowsily slouching down on the couch, and took a deep breath. For something she was so sure she needed, so sure she wanted, she suddenly felt extremely unsure about this new position. But, Della was right. She needed to get back to her own life. She couldn't be expected to stay in Dalesville forever, right?

She clicked "book your ticket," and shut the computer. She fluffed the pillow under Della's head and pulled the knit blanket up under her chin. Even in such a fragile state, Della was beautiful. She was perfect. And though Luci had all the faith in the world in her best friend, her heart was heavy. She curled up next to Della and closed her eyes.

# FIVE
*Della*

"Come on, Luci, we're going to be fighting traffic as it is," Della called up the steps. For someone who had buried her husband a few days before, she was feeling oddly peppy. She knew why; after the pain of losing her parents, she'd become an expert at blocking the unpleasant—or the unbearable—out. Luci would preach how unhealthy it was, that she should talk to someone, that she needed to find a release, but she just wasn't interested. She found she could patch up the gaping wounds with a metaphorical Band-Aid and keep moving on.

Luci appeared at the bottom of the steps, a solemn look on her face and a sigh escaping her lips.

"Stop moping, Luce. I'm going to be fine. You have worked your ass off for this interview. You have to go back." Luci looked down at her feet. "What is it?" Della asked. There was no hiding anything between the two of them.

"I actually. . . I actually already had the

37

interview," Luci said. Oh no. She'd had it? The look on Luci's face was one of concern, and Della knew just what that meant.

"Oh, Luci," she said, grabbing her hand, "I'm so sorry. I can't *believe* they didn't offer it to you! Those stupid idiots! You were the top in your class! You've brought in more business in the last year than any of those bastards—"

"Dell, I got it," Luci said. Della's eyebrows shot up, her jaw dropping.

"You. . . you got it?" she asked, her hands trembling. Luci nodded. Della sprung onto her with the biggest, warmest hug. But she couldn't figure out why her heart felt a little colder. She was so happy for Luciana. She deserved this. She worked so, *so* hard.

But Della couldn't help but notice the sense of permanence the idea of this new job brought. She'd always secretly hoped that Luci would make her way back to the East Coast, once she'd conquered the West. And now that Della was truly alone, she had found herself hoping for it even more. But Luci could never, *ever* know.

"Oh, my God, Luciana! I am so proud of you! When do you start?" she asked, hugging Luci again.

"I'm supposed to start in a few months, after the current VP officially retires," she said.

"'Supposed to?'"

"Yeah. I haven't officially accepted it yet."

Della looked at her, confused.

"Why?"

"Well, I just didn't know how things would be here, and . . ." Luci started to say, shrugging. But Della held her hand up.

"Luce, you have to take it. You have to go back. I will be fine. I'm just so, *so* proud of you." She enveloped her in a long hug once more before they made their way out of the house.

Despite the fact that she was on her way to deliver her best friend to the airport where she would fly thousands of miles away, Della was thankful for the distraction. She needed errands to run, things to get done.

When they pulled up to the airport drop-off, Della tried desperately to swallow the lump in her throat. She couldn't let Luci see her struggle, or she would stay. She would stay and give up everything, and Della would have none of it.

"I'll be back in a couple of weeks, okay?" Luci said. Della nodded with a smile.

"Go get 'em, Luce," was all she could muster up to say for fear of her voice cracking. Luci cracked a pained smile before wrapping her in a long, long hug. "Call me when you land." Della said. Luci nodded.

"Love you, Alled," she said. Della smiled.

"L-Y-L-A-S, Icul," Della said back. Luci giggled. When they were eight, they created code names for each other that were really their first names spelled backwards. They were *so* stealth.

Della watched Luci walk through the huge glass doors, her eyes locked on her until she disappeared.

As Della drove back into Dalesville, she stopped at at one of the traffic lights in town even though it was still green. She could turn left and head back to her empty house. Her house that had been filled with joy, and laughter, and love, just a few days before, but was now filled with nothing but cold memories. Or, she could go into town, grab a coffee, and avoid it all for a bit longer.

She walked into the doors at the Music Café and made her way up to counter.

"Can I get an iced coffee, please?" she asked,

then paused. "Er, uh, better make that decaf."

"Sure thing," the barista said, punching in the numbers and taking Della's credit card.

As she reached for a straw, she felt the sides of her shirt creeping up. She'd be trying to convince herself that she didn't quite need maternity shirts yet, but it was looking more and more like the time had come. She took a seat at one of the tables in a back corner, flipping through her phone as she sipped. She froze when she landed on a picture of Jackson on her Facebook feed.

"Will miss you forever, friend," one post from an old high school friend read. The comments below it delivered individual blows to her stomach, one by one.

*Omg, so sad he won't be here for his baby! :(*

*His poor wife! Thoughts are with her and the baby.*

*Praying that she finds strength. So sorry for your loss!*

She slammed the phone down on the table, as if it itself had personally victimized her. There was a huge knot forming in her stomach, despite the fact that it, along with some of her other organs, was currently being crushed and reformed by the tiny human growing inside of her. She sunk her head down to her hands and took a few deep breaths.

She'd made a deal with herself three days ago that she wouldn't cry in public anymore. So far, she was 0 for 3.

"Della?" she heard a familiar voice say. She shot up quickly, drying her cheeks on her sleeve.

"Dayton, hi," she said, surprised. The look on his face was one she had come to recognize quickly: sympathy. And she was starting to hate it.

"How are you doing?" he asked.

"I'm good, I'm good. Do you want to sit?" she

asked. She didn't know why she offered; the last thing she wanted was interaction right now. But, to her dismay, he pulled out the chair next to her.

"How are you *really* doing?" he asked, crossing his hands on the table and leaning in toward her. She sighed. He had already seen her at her most fragile, moments after she discovered her husband was dead. What was the use in putting up a front now?

"I haven't lived life without him in almost ten years," she said. "And man, I miss him." Dayton nodded.

"I know you do. I do, too." She looked up at him, a pang of guilt beating inside her heart.

"Dayton, you should know something. Even after everything, Jackson always considered you a friend. It killed him not inviting you to our wedding. I suppose that was my fault, but with Luci, I just couldn't—" he held up his hand.

"I always considered him a friend, too. Till the day he. . . till the end. He was honest to God, one of my truest friends. And I always felt like, even if we hadn't talked in months, if I was down-and-out at three a.m., he'd be the one I could call."

She smiled. Dayton was right. Jackson was always, *always* there. She remembered the night they found her father in the ditch. It happened to be the same day that Jackson had gotten his first management role at a technology company a few miles away. Unbeknownst to Della, he had planned to come home from the interview with a bouquet of flowers, letting her know their life together was about to change for the better. Instead, he spent the night on their back porch, her head on his shoulder, her tears on his shirt.

"I don't know if I'll come back from this, Dayton," she said, staring down at her own hands, her wedding band sparkling extra bright on her finger.

"I can't imagine what it must feel like," he said,

sitting back, "the one person you love, you need more than anyone, leaving."

Then he looked down at the ground, as if he were contemplating whether or not he *could* imagine it. Della raised an eyebrow.

"You know, in a way, I think Luci has sort of felt this before," she said. Come on, she couldn't be expected to get through a whole conversation with him without bringing up her best friend, who he absolutely crushed. He didn't even look up at her, just nodded, slowly.

"I owe Luci an explanation," he said.

"That would be nice," Della said. "Do you have her number?" He shook his head.

"No, but I'd really like to do it in person. I owe her that." Della looked down at the ground.

"Well, that might have to wait a while. She's currently in the air, flying back to Seattle."

Dayton's eyes flashed toward her.

"She went back?" he asked, not even attempting to mask the disappointment.

"She did. She had to. She's going to be a vice president of her company," she said with a smile. She sucked down the last bit of decaf coffee, which, in her opinion, was about as useful as a rubber knife. Then she stood up, pulling down on the hem of her shirt again. He rose with her, putting his hand just to her side, as if to guide her. She smiled. Some people were so funny with pregnant women; they treated them like the finest china they owned, which Della could get used to.

"Well, I guess I need to go figure out how to live the rest of my life," she said with a smile, trying to sound casual. Dayton wrapped his arms around her.

"Please, call me if you need anything. You know I'm right up the street."

"Thank you, Dayton," she said.

A few minutes later, Della turned the key to her front door as slowly as ever, then forced herself to step inside. She looked down the basement steps. The couch where Cash had been sleeping was all made up, the blanket folded nice and neat.

The kitchen was spotless, obviously Luci's doing, and in the freezer were four huge trays of lasagna from Mrs. Ruiz. As she chucked her keys into the basket on the entryway table, she took a deep breath.

She was alone. In their house.

She made her way upstairs, taking another breath before she opened their bedroom door. *Her* bedroom door. As she walked past the closets, she stopped when she saw her own reflection. Her eyes were a little droopy, and it seemed like the skin underneath them might have a permanent purple hue to it. But she didn't care.

The bump underneath her too-small shirt took her breath away for a moment. She felt the familiar flutter of some sort of body part moving around, and said a silent prayer of thanks that Jackson had felt it once before the accident.

It first happened two days before Jackson died. Della had felt the baby moving a few times before now, but it was still too deep, too faint for anyone on the outside to feel. But on that particular night, she just knew the little munchkin was strong enough.

Jackson had been in the shower while she was watching *Property Brothers*, chowing down on Chex Mix in their bed. At first, she thought it might be a gas bubble. But then it happened again. The tiniest flutter deep in her belly. And she screamed his name.

Jackson ran from the bathroom, butt-naked, sliding across their hardwood floors.

"What? What happened? Are you hurt? Are you okay?" he asked. She smiled and grabbed his hand, putting it over the fluttering. The panic in his eyes melted away so fast, replaced with the greatest joy she'd ever seen. He laughed a hearty laugh, wrapped his hands around her head, and kissed her.

"That's my baby," he had said, staring down at her belly, and kissing it.

As he turned back toward the bathroom, she had spanked his butt. *Those* were the only man buns she was interested in.

She smiled at the memory, pressing her hand to the spot where her baby, Jackson's baby, was pushing a tiny foot out. She walked over to his closet, yanking her favorite Dalesville High basketball hoodie from his top shelf and pulling it on over her head. But as his scent surrounded her, she felt the most intense feeling of loneliness she'd ever felt. It was like reality was descending now, suffocating her.

And suddenly, the baby inside of her seemed like the scariest being she'd ever come in contact with.

Because she was all alone.

She sank to the floor and pulled her knees up to her belly, crouched amongst his clothes, and finally succumbed to the tears.

# SIX
*Luci*

"So you'll stay in the cubicles for another week, but as soon as they have the walls painted, you'll move into your new office," Mia said as they walked down one of the long hallways and into Mia's office.

Luci's heart skipped a beat. Her own office. With her own view of the Space Needle, way up in the clouds.

"So, you'll just need to go down to HR sometime this week and finish signing your paperwork for the promotion." Mia plopped down on the leather couch in her huge corner office, putting her feet up on the coffee table in front of her. Luci joined her, taking in a deep breath. "You so deserve this, Luciana. You were made for this position. We are so lucky to have you."

Luci smiled. She *did* deserve this. It was her time.

"Thank you for everything, Mia," she said.

"Don't thank me, kid," Mia said, scanning her fingernails. "You put the work in. Thank yourself. I'm a big believer that age isn't everything. There are people

45

who have been in this business for thirty years, but don't have the innate business sense and professionalism that you were born with. You're the real deal, Luciana."

Luci smiled. "Well, I guess I better go get back to my last week in the old spot!" She stood up from the couch, heading toward the door.

"Oh, by the way," Mia said, "how was everything back home? How's your friend doing?" Luci felt her spine straighten immediately. She'd been trying to avoid mixing work with Della. After all, work was the only thing keeping her *from* Della.

"It was. . . it was good to be back. So good to see her. She's doing okay. She's a tough cookie," Luci answered.

"Mmm. And they don't have any leads on the bastard that shot her husband?" Mia asked. Luci shook her head.

"Mmm," Mia went on. "I just can't even imagine. That right there, that's why I don't want a man. Or anyone, really. It's a lot easier to live alone and not have to deal with the fucking heartbreak like that. God," she said, sipping her coffee and standing up from the couch.

The casual tone in Mia's voice was a bit jarring; she spoke as if losing a loved one was totally and completely inevitable; like losing them outweighed the joy of ever having them in the first place.

Nevertheless, Luci smiled, although her heart wasn't in it.

Throughout her time in Seattle, she'd been compared to Mia more times than she could count. Luci was her protégé; Mia made it quite clear that she saw herself in Luci and wanted Luci to follow her footsteps.

But vowing to be forever alone just to avoid heartache wasn't a path Luci was sure she wanted to follow. Even after Jackson. Even after Dayton. Even after her father.

◊

That night, Luci's coworkers took her to dinner to celebrate her last week among the "little people." Becky ordered shot after shot while Jordan kept visiting the DJ, requesting outlandish songs that were impossible to dance to.

"I can't believe you're leaving us," Becky said, taking a break from the dance floor and climbing up into the barstool next to Luci.

"Aw, I know, Beck," Luci said, throwing one more shot back. "I will miss you guys, really."

"All of us?" she heard a familiar voice whisper into her ear. She smiled. Charlie's voice was cool and smooth, like a piece of glass. She particularly liked it when it was saying her name after a night cap in her bedroom. Or in her shower. Or on her dining room table, like last week. She cleared her throat.

"All of you," she said. "But I'll only be one floor away."

Jordan smirked. "One floor away might as well be a thousand miles," he said.

She smiled faintly, thinking of the people who really *were* thousands of miles away.

After a few more painfully weird songs, Luci stood up, pulling her purse up over her shoulder.

"Heading out?" Becky asked.

"Yeah, I'm getting tired," she said. Charlie looked at her, a familiar, hungry look in his eyes. He had a healthy appetite that she was normally very happy to help curb.

"You want some company tonight?" he asked, sneaking his arm tightly around her waist. She smiled.

"Sorry, Charlie," she said, making him cringe. She loved using that saying. "I think I might actually call it a night. I'm really tired."

He looked devastated, like someone had slapped his mother. She had never turned him down, in the entire year that they had been hooking up. He was jaw-droppingly gorgeous; slick brown hair and bright blue eyes. He could pull off a suit better than Christian Grey himself. And she knew he was the catch of the office. But after she'd been home, after she'd seen Della's pain, after she'd seen. . .*him* again, she just wasn't interested. Her libido was currently taking a long vacation.

"Wow, so you climb the corporate ladder and you don't need me anymore?" he said with a chuckle, but she could tell there was hurt behind his words.

"I'm sorry," she said, "it's not like that." She hugged him, kissed Becky's cheek, and waved to Jordan as she walked out to meet her Lyft.

When Luci got back to her apartment, she slipped her shoes off and shimmied out of her tight dress, pulling on a pair of perfectly broken-in Dalesville High sweatpants and a baggy t-shirt. As she sat on her couch, flipping through the channels, a stack of her yearbooks caught her eye on the bookshelf against the back wall. She grabbed her senior yearbook, laying it down on the coffee table in front of the couch, and turned the pages.

She and Della had been featured on the "best friends forever" page, with a picture of them in second grade next to a picture of them as seniors. She smiled, running her fingers over the picture. She flipped a few more pages, until she came across a long note written sideways down one page.

*Icul,*

*I cannot believe this is it! We are SENIORS! Gosh, it feels like we were just chasing Peter Grady at our fifth grade picnic. How did we even get here?! I just wanted to let you know how special you are to me, and how thankful I am for you. Friendships like ours don't come around every day, and I am so grateful for it. I know that no matter where we end up in life, we will always have each other. And I hope you know that no matter what, I will always, ALWAYS be here for you. I love you!*

*LYLAS,*
*Your Alled*


It tore at Luci's heart that when Della wrote this, she didn't have a worry in the world. She had Luci, she had her mom and dad, she had Jackson, and they were just starting to plan out their lives together. Little did she know, just a few short years later, she'd be all alone, starting from ground zero.

Except she didn't have to be alone. Luci was still here. She was still around. She could be there.

She scrambled to her phone. She needed to hear Della's voice. She needed some reassurance that her best friend really was okay.

"Hello?" Della answered.

"Hi, sorry I'm calling so late. Were you asleep?"

"Nope, not even close. It's Harry Potter weekend, so I'm not doing anything but watching T.V.," Della said. "So, tell me about it! When do you start the new position?"

Luci paused for a moment. Even though she was feigning excitement, Luci could tell there was something in Della's voice. Something off.

"Next week," Luci said, desperate to change the subject, "but how are you doing?"

There was a silence on the other end of the line.

"Dell?"

"I'm. . . I'm okay," she finally said.

"What's going on?" Luci asked.

"Well, I got a call from the doctor today, and I have to schedule my anatomy scan and sonogram for my appointment next week."

"Okay. . . isn't that a good thing?"

Another silence. Then she heard sniffling.

"Dell? What is it? What's wrong?"

"This is the scan where we. . .where I find out the gender. Without Jackson."

Luci felt her heart ripping in two.

"Oh, Della. . ." was all she could muster up. Now there was sniffling coming from both ends of the line. Luci sank to the floor in front of her couch, pulling her knees up to her chest. For a moment they said nothing. Then Della spoke, lightly, wearily.

"It's okay, I'll be okay. . . I just, I just never thought I'd be doing this without him. I think I'm going to try and get some sleep. I'll call you tomorrow."

"Okay, night, Dell. Love you," Luci said, her lip quivering.

"Love you, too."

As she finally let the tears loose, Luci knew exactly what she was going to do. What she had to do. She picked her phone up again and dialed Mia.

"Hello? Luciana? Is everything okay?" Mia asked.

"Yes, I'm so sorry to call so late," she said. "But I have something really important to talk to you about."

"Okay?"

"I can't take the job," Luci blurted out. There was a long, stomach-twisting silence.

"Meet me at Purple Café in fifteen minutes," Mia said, then hung up. Luci sighed. She knew this wouldn't be easy.

She threw on presentable clothes, suddenly wondering why she had to make that call now instead of the next morning, and cursing her impulsivity for forcing her to put a bra back on. She trudged outside, hailed a cab, and hopped out in front of the restaurant a few minutes later.

"Sit," was all Mia said as she sipped her martini. Luci sat. "So what is this all about?" Luci sighed.

"Well, I talked to Della tonight, and I. . ."

"Oh, goodness," Mia muttered, rolling her eyes and rubbing her temples. Suddenly, a fire started inside of Luci.

"You know, you don't know anything about Della, or our friendship, or—" Luci started on her defense, but Mia cut her off.

"No, I don't, you're right. And I don't need to. Look, Luciana, women like us, we can have it all. We can be the change makers in our world. But we have to work our asses off to do it. I know you love this industry. And you, especially, being from *your* background? Everything you've been through? And on top of that, you're *damn* good at your job. I understand that your friend is hurting. She's in pain, and it's sadly a pain that no one, not even you, can fix for her. And you know what? A few months from now, she'll be better. She'll be exhausted as all hell—I don't know *why* people have children on purpose—but she will be better. And then what? What about you? You're just essentially a stay-at-home mom without her own kid? Or you get a boring job that pays half as much? Let all your potential go to waste?"

Luci just sat there, staring blankly ahead with her jaw dropped. Honestly, she had no idea what the fuck to say. She hadn't gotten that far in her plans. Mia was asking all the same questions Luci had been avoiding asking herself. Questions she definitely did not have the answers to just yet. But it was fine, because *luckily* Mia wasn't finished yet.

"Luci, it's *okay* for women to not want kids. It's *okay* to not want to settle down. It's *okay* to just want a kick-ass career. It's *okay* to be a little bit selfish now and then to get what we deserve. I just don't want you to lose sight of that."

After a moment, Luci nodded and cleared her throat.

"I get what you're saying, Mia, really. And I don't want you to think I'm ungrateful for the opportunities you've given me over the years. But Della, she's more than my friend. She's my family. She needs me. And I can't think of anything else that matters more than that."

Mia looked at her through squinty eyes, taking one last, drawn-out sip of her drink before gently putting the glass back on the table.

"Alright," she finally said, "here's the deal. Rodney doesn't retire for another three months. I can give you one month to figure this out. I can give you one month to figure out where you want to be. After that, I'll need to open the position back up to interviews. In the meantime, you can work remotely."

Luci raised her eyebrows in disbelief. Was that all some twisted test? A quick smile flashed across Mia's face.

"Now, go be with your friend," she said.

# SEVEN
*Della*

The obnoxious sound of her alarm sent her springing up as if the house was on fire. Though, if it were, she swore she'd probably burn to a crisp. The ever-growing belly was making it harder and harder to move around each day. When she caught her breath, she swung her legs over the side of the bed, letting them dangle for a moment.

A few weeks earlier, Jackson had convinced her that they needed a king-sized bed.

"Come on, babe. We're always pushing each other to the edge as it is, and it's just going to get more squishy when the baby gets bigger and is in our bed. And can you imagine when we have more? This bed is going to be *way* too small."

The memory made her shudder, thinking about all the other children that they would never have. Now, the king bed seemed way too big; like it threatened to swallow her whole every night when she got into it.

As she trudged across the bedroom and slid into

her slippers, tying her robe around her belly, she wondered why she even set the alarm in the first place. She wasn't working, she had nowhere to be, no one to see.

But the tiny kicks came from her belly, ordering womb service, so she made her way down the half-flight of stairs into the kitchen. She stood up on her tip-toes in the cabinet, reaching for the canister of oatmeal that Jackson always put on the top shelf, forgetting that she ate it, too. As she reached, she found that her belly pushed her out further, making it even more difficult to reach. But finally, with one more push and a wiggle of her fingers, she got it.

She leaned against the counter as it cooked in the microwave, scrolling through her phone.

*Heard this song on the radio today, and thought about you immediately. Miss you, my friend,* Ben Knoxville's post read. The video posted was of Knox and Jackson dancing, in their full football gear, in the middle of the field during halftime of one of their high school games. She smiled as she watched, not even realizing she was crying until she tasted the salt of her tears on her lips.

For the most part, these types of posts, memories, cards, even calls, had dissipated. The meal trains had stopped, and she was down to her last few frozen dinners.

In some ways, it was a relief. She could continue moping around the house in Jackson's clothes, not showering for a few days at a time, until she actually started to stink. She was Hillary Swank in *P.S. I Love You.* The smelly widow who refused to wash any clothes—or herself—for fear of losing another piece of her dead husband.

But in other ways, the lack of human contact was completely devastating. She didn't care about the attention; she didn't want to be the subject of conversation around town anymore, and she was *so* freaking sick of all the damn puppy-dog eyes full of sorrow and sympathy. But what she *did* care about was the fact that it felt like Jackson was getting lost.

Not to her, of course. She couldn't turn a corner without being smacked in the face with some sort of memory of him. But everyone else around her was moving on with their lives, leaving Jackson in the past.

She clicked her phone screen off and grabbed the oatmeal from the microwave, stirring it.

But something stopped her dead in her tracks. She felt sick to her stomach instantly. For a moment, she wondered if it was the post, seeing her Jackson in action again. But as she brought the bowl closer to her face, she quickly realized it was the oatmeal.

Suddenly her trusty breakfast staple had become the enemy.

She scraped the entire bowl into the trash can, then plugged her nose again. The worst smell she could have ever imagined was now pouring into the air from the can. She was pretty sure something had crawled in during the middle of the night and died. Holy shit. She hadn't taken the trash out since Cash left. Jesus, she hadn't taken the trash out *ever*. Jackson had always done that.

As she jumped back, her phone buzzed.

"Hey, C," she said, still holding her nose closed.

"Are you okay? Why's your voice all weird?" Cash asked.

"Well, I realized that in order for the trash to be taken out, someone must *actually* take it out. God, I was really spoiled. I swear to God I don't even know where our outdoor trash cans are," she said, putting the phone on speaker and laying it down on the counter. Cash chuckled.

"They are out on the side of the back deck," he said. She smiled. Of course he knew. He'd taken it out every time it filled up since Jackson died.

"Thanks," she said. "So what's up?"

"Nothing much. Just checking in on you. How's my niece-slash-nephew doing?" he asked.

"He-she is doing great. Hungry. But apparently he-she doesn't like oatmeal, so I'm currently trying to figure out what he-she *does* like these days. Doesn't seem to be much," she said. Cash laughed again.

"Okay, well I'm meeting up with Sharelle to go over our study guide for my Sociology exam next week. I'll check in on you tomorrow," he said.

"Sharelle, huh? Is this the same girl you studied with last week?" she asked. She could practically hear him smiling through the phone.

"Yes, Della, it is," he said. "Now go do something fun today. I'll talk to you soon. Love you."

"Love you, too. And Cash?"

"Yeah?"

"Be a gentleman, okay?"

"Always."

She walked back toward the pantry, drumming her fingers against the door as she scanned every single thing in the cabinet. Luci's mom had stocked it the day after the funeral with enough canned and boxed food to last her a lifetime, yet, somehow, not a damn thing looked good. She finally settled on a jar of creamy peanut butter and a spoon. As she made her way toward the couch, she heard a car door shut outside. Thank God she hadn't sat down yet, or else she probably wouldn't have been able to get to the door when the unexpected visitor actually knocked.

As she dragged her feet to the big window in the front room, her jaw dropped, and her hand fell limp, sending the jar of peanut butter crashing to the floor. Della ran to the front door and yanked it open.

Outside stood Luci, leaning against her own car, with three of her huge suitcases. The inside of her car was loaded from top to bottom with stuff. Luci pushed herself upright off the side of her car.

"I heard you were looking for a new roommate," she said, a huge smile breaking out on her face. "How much is rent?"

"*What?*" was all Della could say, her voice quivering and her hands shaking. She sprung down the porch steps and ran to Luci, careful not to bump her belly. "What are you *doing* here? How did you *get* here?" she asked. Luci wrapped her arms around her, squeezing her tightly.

"I've been driving for the last three days. I want to be here for you," she said. "I don't want to miss all of this." She put her hands on Della's bump.

"Luci. . ." she started to protest, but Luci just shook her head.

"Stop, Della. I *want* to be here. I promise."

Della stared at her, squeezing Luci's hands tight. She loved that they could have a whole conversation without actually having to speak words. She wanted to protest more. She knew a good friend would push Luci to go back to the career she had worked her *ass* off for. She knew she should tell her to go back to Seattle, the city she had fallen in love with, and live the life she had wanted for so long.

But as she stood there in front of her house with her best friend in her arms again, she couldn't do it. She had to be selfish. She had to keep her. The truth was, she wasn't sure how she was going to do it all without Jackson.

She'd been telling everyone for weeks that she was going to be fine, and that she was ready for the baby. But in the quiet of an empty house, she knew she was fooling herself.

She knelt down to grab the smaller of the suitcases while Luci grabbed the two bigger ones. She helped carry the lighter things inside as Luci grabbed all the big stuff. Della couldn't help but notice how in shape Luci was. Wasn't Seattle supposed to be perpetually rainy? Yet somehow, Luci had a nice tan that complemented her deep, dark locks. The muscles in her arms flexed each time she bent down to pick something up, and Della looked down at her own arms. She'd noticed over the past couple of weeks that her arms seemed to be getting a little bit more jiggly, as if everything she ate went directly to them.

She was also pretty sure that she had more neck fat than the week before. Pregnancy was unforgiving.

Luci had always been a workout-a-holic; she'd been a swimmer in high school and took up kickboxing and Zumba when they graduated. Della, on the other hand, preferred to take her naturally small frame for granted, refusing to break a sweat unless it was absolutely necessary. She had been able to eat whatever her heart desired, and never gain a pound. Yet, their whole lives, they had been able to share clothes. Now, Della almost snorted at the idea of squeezing into Luci's wardrobe.

She'd like to see what she'd look like now, pregnant belly and all, in the racerback tank and leggings that Luci had on. Probably like a busted can of uncooked biscuits.

After a few hours of moving Luci's things into the guest room and organizing them somewhat, they both plopped down on the couch.

"Wanna get some grub?" Della asked. "Sorry I'm not the best hostess." Luci shot her a look.

"First of all, I *always* want grub," she said. "And

secondly, you're not a hostess. We're roommates. That is, if you'll have me."  Now Della shot Luci a look.

"No way. Get out now," she said. Luci rolled her eyes and stuck her tongue out.

"I need some Tom and Ray's," Luci said, pushing herself up from the couch, then sticking her hands out to Della to pull her up.


As they walked into the restaurant, Della could see Luci's face lighting up. They had come here almost every day during their senior year of high school when they had open lunch, and after all of Jackson's football games. Their favorite appetizer was fries with gravy. They loved the looks they got from the wait staff whenever they ordered it.

"Gravy? Like, the gravy that goes with our Salisbury steak?" the teenage server with a Mohawk and a bullring in his nose asked, as if they were the ones with something sticking out of *their* faces.

"Yep. That's the stuff," Luci said, handing him her menu.

"I'll have a slice of cheesecake, and a side of broccoli," Della said. Now, the server looked at them as if they weren't speaking English. And Luci was staring at her, too. "What? This baby has the weirdest pallet, I swear." Luci laughed.

"You heard the girl," she told the waiter.

"So," Della said, "tell me how this all came about. I mean, don't get me wrong, I couldn't be more excited to have you here. God knows, I was beginning to freak the fuck out about doing this all on my own. But you have a whole *life* there. And that job? Oh, God! You didn't take it, did you?" she asked, feeling the panic of ruining someone else's life taking over her voice, making it all squeaky and crackly. Luci smiled and squeezed her hand.

"Della, I'm here because I *want* to be. There are some things, and some people, that are more important than anything else. Besides, it's not necessarily permanent. I just want to spend a little more time with you. Help you out when you need it. They are giving me some time to decide if I want to take it. I'm fine. Okay?"

Della took a breath and nodded slowly.

"Luci?" Della heard a familiar voice ask, and she watched as Luci's spine straightened, as if she'd been electrocuted. "You're back," Dayton said.

Della's eyes flashed from Dayton to Luci, back to Dayton, then back to Luci. She couldn't take the awkward silence anymore.

"How are you, Dayton?" she asked, instinctively reaching out and grabbing for his hand, forgetting that she was supposed to hate his stinking guts.

"I'm good, Della, thanks. How are you feeling?" He asked her, but the whole time, she watched as his eyes searched desperately for Luci's face out of their corners.

"I'm feeling good. Better, now that my new roomie is here," she said. She watched as Luci shot daggers at her, but she kept going. "Luci here has postponed her *amazing* west coast life to help her widowed best friend through her next trimester, bless her heart."

"Wow," Dayton said, his eyes flicking back to Luci. "That's really awesome of you."

"Yeah, well, that's what you do for the people you love. You're there for them. You don't abandon them," Luci said, crossing her arms on top of the table. Dayton looked down at the ground.

"Right," he said quietly. "Look, Luci, since you're going to be around, I was wondering if we might be able to. . . catch up. . ." he asked, letting his voice trail off.

"You're about three years too late in asking me

that," she said, and everything grew quiet. Luci looked from Della, to Dayton, to the food that was now growing cold on the table. Dayton cleared his throat and nodded, making his way to the bar. Della shot Luci a look.  Even though Dayton had wiggled his way back into Della's heart, it was clear that Luci's was still on lockdown.

"I have to pee," Della said, scooting her way out of the booth. When she finally wriggled the bump free of the squishy booth, she made her way to Dayton.

"Don't worry," she whispered as she walked by him. "She'll come around."

# EIGHT
*Luci*

She knew she could go a little easier on him, but she didn't want to. Screw that. He'd left her sitting, like some hopeless idiot, on her parents' front porch. Waiting for him to take her out for the "special night" he had planned, waiting for him to ask her the *most* important question.

He'd just graduated from the police academy a few months before, and he'd been talking a lot about their future.

She was finished with school, and was fully committed to the job-hunt in D.C. and Baltimore, trying to find *something* close to Dalesville so they wouldn't have to move. After all, Dayton wanted to be a Moore County cop since fifth grade.

He'd been acting weird for the past week, and she felt like everyone around her was in on a secret that she wasn't. And everyone around her just happened to be *horrible* at keeping secrets. Her mother was avoiding her, and even her father wouldn't accept her FaceTime calls. But the clincher was when Della canceled on her.

Della had a hard time keeping her mouth shut in general, but with Luci, she didn't even need to speak. It was the years of experience that Luci had with Della. . . there were absolutely no secrets between them, even if Della wanted there to be.

So, the night rolled around, and Dayton had told her to be out on her front porch by 7:15. Two days before, Della had made her an appointment for a manicure, as an early birthday present, despite the fact that Luci's birthday wasn't for another two months. Subtle.

Luci sat on the front steps, wearing her favorite burgundy dress that hugged her waist but wasn't *too* tight. She wore black strappy sandals, tried straightening her thick curls, and wore just a little bit more makeup that day than normal. Her heart pounded in her chest as she waited for the rumbling of his truck.

She tapped her foot nervously. This was it. After tonight, she would be officially off the market. But the thought didn't scare her. Not in the least. In fact, she couldn't wait.

There was so much about their future that they were unsure about. Where they'd live, what she'd do for a living. . . but this? This was a no-brainer. She knew she was supposed to be with Dayton for the rest of her life.

She was supposed to grow old with him. They were supposed to go on double-dates with Della and Jackson. They were supposed to travel together. Maybe someday, they'd settle down and maybe, *maybe,* have a family of their own.

But it was all supposed to happen with him.

After an hour and three calls that went straight to his voicemail, Luci was getting really worried. Just as she was about to dial Jackson to see if he'd heard from Dayton, she saw Della's little white Dodge pull up in front of her parents' house. At first, Luci's heart had fluttered. Maybe this was part of the surprise. Maybe he was having all of the people she loved show up one-by-one. But as Della emerged from the car, face pale with some sort of uneasy emotion, Luci knew this was not part of any plan.

"Dell? What's going on?" she asked. As Della walked up to the front walk, she paused at the mailbox. She opened it, and when she laid her eyes on whatever was inside, she closed them for a moment, letting out a long, slow breath.

"Della? What is going on? Where is he?"

Della grabbed the letter from the mailbox and walked up the porch steps, motioning for Luci to sit back down. She handed her the letter, waiting patiently as she read it.

*Dear Luci,*

*I wish there was more I could tell you. I wish there was a reason I could give you that would be worthy of you. But there's not.*

*I know at this point, these next few words probably mean nothing. But you need to know that you are everything to me. I love you, and I always will.*

*I'm sorry, Luci.*

*You deserve so much more, and I'll be praying every day that you get it.*

*Dayton*

She read the shortest, vaguest, most unhelpful letter in the history of letters six times before looking up at Della, her hands trembling.

"What?" she asked. Della's eyes dropped to the ground as she scooted closer to Luci, wrapping an arm around her shoulders.

"I'm so sorry, Luce," she whispered.

"*What?*" Luci asked again, feverishly rereading the words he'd scratched down. She was gripped with fear and anger. How was it possible for her to lose the love of her life, the night she was supposed to promise herself to him forever?

"I don't know, Luci, I'm so sorry," Della said, wrapping her other arm around Luci now, and pulling her in close. "He just called Jackson and told him to have me come here. He said to check the mailbox. He said he couldn't explain it, but he was sorry."

Luci could feel her whole body starting to shake.

For a few weeks afterward, she'd done a pretty good job of not contacting him. God knows she wanted to; she had rolled over and snatched up her phone so many times in the middle of the night, then slammed it back down.

Once, though, she couldn't help it. She had to hear his voice. She needed to hear him say out loud that it was really over. Despite the fact that she'd recognize his chicken-scratch handwriting anywhere, she was half-convinced he had written it by force. Someone had a gun to his head. Probably Joanna. Luci always suspected that Joanna wasn't quite over him.

She dialed him late one night, sitting out on the porch swing of her parents' house. It rang three times, then went to voicemail.

A minute later, a text came through.

*I'm sorry, Luci,* was all it said. She promised herself then and there that she would do whatever it took to move on. In fact, for a while, she'd sworn off men altogether. The ones she loved either got shipped thousands of miles away from her, or left her behind with no explanation.

But each time she'd seen him since she'd been back in Dalesville was just a painful reminder that she had failed. She'd been with a handful of other men, but nothing even came close. And she hated that.

Every time she laid eyes on him, she was hit with a fresh wave of the same pain she felt the night he left. And as much as she'd like to say she wanted him to feel that same pain, she knew it would be a lie. Because the only thing worse than the pain she felt, would be seeing *him* in pain. She hated that, too.

"You know," Della said, as they strolled down the sidewalk, "you should go a little easier on him." Luci rolled her eyes. "I'm serious. He's been really good to me with everything. He was the first one on the scene, he was the first one who told me, he's the only one who still shows up to check on me."

At that, Luci held back a bit. He was still the same old, nauseatingly sweet Dayton.

"I'm glad he's been here for you," she said. "But I can't even look at him." And she meant it. Although she could admittedly look at his perfect face all damn day, it brought her nothing but pain.

"Well, maybe you should just hear him out. It might help you get some closure, if nothing else," she said, reaching her hand out to squeeze Luci's arm.

"I don't even want to know why, at this point," Luci said. "I just want to move on."

Della snorted.

"What?" Luci snapped back.

"This is me you're talking to. We both know you will never be okay with not knowing. You have to know *everything,*" she said. "I mean, it was completely out of the blue. He was *so* ready to marry you. And the ring was—" she stopped, realizing she had said too much.

"You saw the ring?" Luci asked, and she felt her heart sink. Della swallowed audibly.

"Yeah. I went with him to pick it out," she said her voice getting quiet with shame.

"You never told me that," Luci said.

"What good would that have done?" Della asked, matter-of-factly. "It doesn't make any sense. There *had* to be a reason, a *real* reason, why he left you. So, I say, tell him you'll meet up with him. And stop being such a cranky bitch."

"You're lucky you're pregnant," Luci said, "because if not, I'd totally be tackling you right about now."

"Whatever. I would still win, pregnant belly and all."

"Look, you're getting soft on me. What about all those years of you saying 'come on, Luci, try to think about something else,' or 'don't let him ruin your happiness,' 'he doesn't deserve you,' remember all that?"

"Yeah, well, I was pissed. Just like you would have been for me. But I don't know, maybe the whole dead husband thing has changed my perspective on second chances," she said. Luci looked up at her.

"Wow, you're going to use the widow card already?" she asked with a smile. Della let out a giggle.

"Hey, it's in the widow's rule book. You get to use the card immediately," Della said, shrugging. Luci chuckled.

"Ah, okay, sorry, I guess I need to brush up on my widow rules."

Just as they were rounding the corner to the parking lot, they stopped dead in their tracks.

"Mrs. Niles?" the voice said, and Luci could feel panic streaking through Della at the mere sound of the voice. It was that young woman from Dayton's funeral. The one he died saving.

"Cora?" Della asked. The young woman looked nervous; she wrapped her arms around herself, swallowing.

"Yes, hi, it's so nice to see you again," Cora said, her voice dripping with shaky anxiety. Luci waited for Della to respond, but she said nothing. She just sank back on her heel, putting one hand to her lower back, the signature pregnant woman stance. When Cora realized that the sentiment wasn't shared, she began digging through her bag, and went on.

"Mrs. Niles, I've actually been hoping to run into you. I have this letter, and I—" Cora started again, holding up an envelope. But Della held up her hand, cutting the poor girl off.

"I'm not interested in your letter," Della said, her voice cold, unfamiliar to Luci. Cora swallowed again, the envelope shaking in her hand. She nodded slowly, her eyebrows knitted together as if she were in pain. Luci reached her hand out, taking the letter from Cora's hand.

"I'm Luci, Della's best friend. We will take this with us, and Della will take a look when she's ready," she said, trying to bring a little bit of civility back into the conversation. Cora nodded again slowly, her eyes darting from Luci, back to the ground, careful not to make contact with Della.

"Thank you, so, so much," Cora said. "Well, it was nice running into you. I hope to hear from you soon," she said, briskly walking past them as she made her way back down Main Street.

Once she was out of earshot, Luci turned to look at Della, arms crossed, foot tapping.

"Okay, who's the cranky bitch now?" she asked, raising an eyebrow. Della sighed and rolled her eyes.

"Forgive me for not wanting to chit-chat with the woman who got my husband killed," she said, turning to walk toward the car.

"Okay, fine, I get it. But let me ask you this," Luci said, reaching for her hand. "Are you telling me, honestly, that you wish Jackson hadn't helped her that night? That you wish he'd just seen it happen, and moved on, letting that man do God knows what to that girl? Is that what you would have wanted?"

Luci watched as Della's eyes bounced back and forth across the pavement, as if she were weighing her options. Like she was running through every possible scenario of that night. Finally, Luci sighed.

"No. No, I'm not telling you that. I'm just. . . I don't know. I guess I just don't really have anything to say to her yet. It's just. . . it's easy to blame her," Della admitted. Luci wrapped an arm around her shoulder before they got into the car.

"I know, Dell. But the truth is, it's not her fault," Luci said.

"Ugh, okay. Enough about Cora, and Jackson, and that night. Back to Dayton," Della said, sliding into the car as gracefully as possible with her bump. Luci giggled and rolled her eyes.

"Ugh, no, enough about Dayton, too. We have *much* more important things to worry about. Like this sonogram that's coming up! I just know it's a girl. I already cannot wait to buy the most frilly, obnoxiously pink things. All pink *everything!*" she said. Della smiled, putting both hands on her belly and looking down at it.

"Jackson always said he knew it was a boy. But I really think it's a girl, too," she said. Luci couldn't help but notice that there sounded like a twinge of disappointment in Della's voice.

The next morning, Luci was bouncing off the walls with excitement.

"Let's go, let's go! We're going to be late!" she sang, running from room to room in the house, grabbing her keys, her purse, and Della's bag.

"Slow your roll, there," Della said, groggily

making her way toward Luci's car.

"Come on! This is going to be one of the best days of your life," Luci said, starting the car and pulling out onto the road. But she could tell from the look in her friend's eyes, that she didn't share that same sentiment.

At the office, Luci took a seat in the waiting room while Della was called back for a quick exam before the sonogram. After a few minutes that seemed to last a few years, a nurse technician stepped out from behind the door.

"Mr. Niles? Your wife will be getting her sonogram now, if you want to come on back," she said, without even looking up from her clipboard. "Mr. Niles?" she asked again, finally looking up to scan the room. Luci stood up and marched over to her.

"I'm here with Mrs. Niles today," she said. The nurse tech looked her up and down once with a peculiar look on her face.

"Oh, and where is Mr. Niles today? Pretty big appointment to miss," she said, loud enough so that everyone in the waiting room could hear. As Luci felt her face grow red, she caught a glimpse of Della through a crack in the door, sitting on the table in the room, her paper gown all crooked. She looked so sad, so lost, on a day when she should be so happy.

"Mr. Niles won't be at any more appointments," Luci said, just above a whisper as she took a threatening step closer to the woman. "Mr. Niles is dead. Now if you'll excuse me," she said, pushing past her toward Della's room, leaving her to pick up her jaw off the floor.

"Okay," the same nurse tech said a few moments later, following her into the room with much more chip in her voice, and much less judgment. "I'm just going to lay the table back some, and the sonographer will be in in just a moment."

"Thank you," Della said.

"So, you ready?" Luci asked, taking Della's hand.

"I guess so," Della said, staring ahead at the blank screen. The sonographer stepped in quickly enough that Luci wasn't forced to desperately conjure a way to brighten the occasion. She lathered Della's belly with some sort of gross jelly, and began waving her magic wand over it.

"Okay, so we're learning the sex today, right?" she asked as she squinted up at the screen.

"Right!" Luci called before Della could answer.

"Okay, are you ready?" the sonographer asked. After a long pause, Della nodded. "Mrs. Niles, congratulations. It's a boy. See there? That's his penis."

"Oh, my gosh! A boy! Look at his little thingy!" Luci exclaimed, jumping up and down and moving closer to the screen. She turned to gauge Della's reaction, just in time to see two crocodile tears rolling down her cheeks.

"Okay," the sonographer said, wiping the goop from Della's belly, "at your next appointment, we will need to do your glucose testing to check for gestational diabetes. You can schedule that up front."

"Hey," Luci said, as they made their way out of the building, "you okay?" Della smiled and nodded, wrapping her hands around her belly.

"He was right," Della whispered. Luci smiled and squeezed her.

# Fall, Third Trimester

# NINE
*Della*

She pushed herself up from her bed, but it was a struggle. The doctors told her to sleep on her left side, not her back or her right side. Something with blood flow to the baby, or something to that effect. All she knew was, she had to totally change her sleeping habits, and it wasn't easy. The baby had become extremely active over the last week, as if he was celebrating his newly discovered anatomy.

She was really enjoying referring to him as "he," and "him," rather than Jackson's favorite "it."

Jackson.

Every thought she had, even the most miniscule, seemed to involve him. Somehow, he crept into every scenario, and it killed her a little bit each time. Like a piece of her heart was chiseled away with each thought of him that snuck into her head.

Luci had been getting up early so she could get to the cafe in town and work for a few hours, so Della had been alone most mornings. Despite the deafening silence that filled her house, she was starting to appreciate the hours of alone time. She didn't have to mask her feelings, her all-consuming heartbreak. She could be devastated for a little bit while she was alone.

She made her way to the kitchen where Luci had left a plate covered in foil and a sticky note that read "EAT THIS." Della uncovered it, stifling a gag from the smell of eggs and bacon. Bleh. Luci had been giving her crap about not getting enough protein, but so many things were making her sick, all she could stand to eat were carbs.

"You're going to make my baby a little shrimp," Luci had told her, shoving Greek yogurt in her face. She thought she was going to hurl.

She scraped the disgusting contents into the trash can, then untwisted the bag of bread and took a bite of two pieces at once. Yes, that would do. Carbs were her friend.

She flipped through the channels, somehow landing on an episode of *Dr. Phil* featuring a widow who swore she could connect with her husband from beyond the grave. Before, she'd have scoffed and flipped the channel. Today, she watched the whole damn episode and sobbed.

After the late morning weep fest, Della went upstairs to change . She made sure to put on real human clothes by lunch time each day, so that Luci wouldn't discover her secretly depressing, pajama-clad mornings. But as she stepped toward her bedroom, she paused at the door next to hers and Jackson's. She hadn't stepped foot in the soon-to-be nursery since Jackson had died. She took a breath and turned the silver doorknob.

The room was small, the smallest of their three bedrooms, but it was perfect. The window faced their backyard, a perfect view of their gigantic oak tree. The first thing they had done was clean out all the pre-baby clutter, so now the room sat perfectly empty, with boring, tan paint on the walls. Despite the memories, she smiled. But as she turned to walk back out of the room, she paused when she saw a piece of paper folded up, sitting on the floor in the back corner of the room.

She spread her legs to get some balance, then leaned down to her right side—this was the most effective way to bend with the belly.

She unfolded it, and almost fell to the ground. She steadied herself against the wall and held the paper in front of her, hands shaking.

He had drawn out an entire blueprint of the nursery, complete with a list of possible paint colors for the walls.

He had scribbled in a drawing of the crib, the changing table, the dresser, even the diaper pail, and she couldn't help but smile through the welling tears. Jackson was so ready to be a father, and that both thrilled and killed her.

Just as she reached up to wipe her nose on her robe sleeve, she felt an arm around her shoulders.

Luci appeared, leaning over and resting her chin on Della's shoulder.

"What's that?" Luci asked.

"It's a blueprint of what he wanted to do for the nursery," Della whispered. "I just found it in here. Never saw it before."

Luci let out a little gasp, reaching for the piece of paper and studying it intently.

"Well," she said after a few moments, and blinking out a few tears of her own, "you are officially more than halfway through the pregnancy. I'd say it's time we get started on this."

Della smiled back. Jackson was her guardian angel, and Luci was her angel on Earth.

The next morning, Luci woke Della much earlier than she had gotten used to waking up, with the pleasant reminder that she couldn't eat, and that her glucose test was this morning.

"Here," she said. "You have to drink this whole thing in seven minutes. It looks like they gave you orange flavor."

She handed her a small bottle of clear liquid. It wasn't huge. . . it couldn't be *that* bad, she told herself.

She unscrewed the cap, slowly moving it toward her lips.

"Don't do it so slow!" Luci said. "You'll smell it and psych yourself out. I'm starting the time in three, two, one. Go!"

Della squeezed her eyes shut and put the top of the bottle to her lips, letting the thick liquid slide into her mouth and ooze down her throat. It tasted like a bottle of Koolaid that had about four cups of sugar and two cups of salt mixed in. This made the eggs and bacon from yesterday seem like a dream. She fought back a gag and Luci screwed her face all up in solidarity.

"Is it bad?" Luci asked, but Della ignored her. She finally pulled the bottle away from her mouth, realizing she'd only drank half of it. Holy shit. This was *awful*.

"You're halfway done! Still have three minutes. You can do this!" Luci cried. If she didn't want to punch someone, Della would have laughed.

She took a few more big gulps, pausing to belch and take a breather.

Three, two, one. *Finally.*

"Ugh," was all Della said as she slammed the empty bottle down on her end table.

At the doctor's office, Della smiled faintly as Luci walked up to the counter to sign her in. It was funny how quickly she'd assumed the role of Della's caretaker, her partner.

Luci held out her hand for Della to squeeze as she got her blood drawn, having learned a few appointments prior just how much Della hated needles.

And Luci pulled up her own calendar on her phone when the woman at the front desk asked Della what day she wanted to come in for her next appointment.

But when they got home, Della noticed that Luci didn't seem quite as excited to scurry to the fridge and put up the newest sonogram photos. She didn't seem as excited to catch up on *Grey's Anatomy.* And she didn't take her typical workout break that day.

Della gave it till after dinner—an awkward, quiet one, at that—before calling her out.

"So, what gives?" she asked, letting Luci stand and collect her dishes, something Della suddenly realized she had grown accustomed to over the last few weeks.

"What do you mean?"

"Well," Della said, scraping her index finger around the rim of her mashed potato bowl before Luci snatched it up, "in all twenty-two years that we've been friends, you've never once skipped a workout. You've been weird all day. So what's up?"

Luci said nothing, just turned the water on full blast in the sink and began scrubbing feverishly at the dishes. Della let her have a moment before standing up, making her way to the sink, and turning it off. She leaned against the counter, crossing her arms over her bump, and raising an eyebrow. Luci smiled faintly and sighed.

"I guess I just realized that this baby is coming soon, and I just don't know... I just don't know what the next few months look like for me."

Della nodded.

"Well," she said, "I imagine you'll be back in Seattle, killing it as the new VP of Millerston Enterprises. Right?"

Luci smiled and nodded.

"Luci, you know how much I love having you here, right?" Della asked. Luci nodded again. "But you know that I could never forgive myself if you gave your life up for me, right? I mean, Jesus, you graduated from high school a semester early, college a *year* early at the top of your class, leadership position by age twenty-four—" Della was interrupted by Luci giggling.

"Geez, Dell, you sound like my freakin' resume," she said. But Della didn't even crack a smile. Luci's success was no laughing matter to her.

"Well, I'm serious. What you've done before the age of thirty is more than most people will achieve by the time they retire. You can't do anything to screw that up just for me."

Luci leaned back against the counter and reached an arm out to droop around Della's shoulders.

"Della, work can wait. Mia is being great about all this, really. I have time before I need to. . . make any changes. My place is here right now." Della nodded, resting her head on Luci's shoulder. As much as she would preach to Luci that her place was in Seattle, another part of her wanted to drop to her knees and beg Luci to stay forever. She wouldn't, though, mostly because she knew just how hard it would be to get back up again.

"Well," Luci said, walking toward the door and grabbing her running shoes, "I guess I will get a quick run in, after all."

# TEN
## *Luci*

Usually, a good workout put Luci in a better mood whenever she was in a shitty one. But tonight, that didn't seem to be the case. It didn't matter how far or how fast she was going, she couldn't outrun the fact that she'd have to make the biggest decision of her professional career in less than a week. If she took this job, she'd be set. Even if she moved to another company eventually, she'd likely never have to settle for less than six figures.

It didn't help that Della was so amazing about it. You'd think it would, but it didn't. It actually made it harder. If Della had seemed totally overwhelmed, overly depressed, totally out of her element, or desperate for Luci to stay, it would make the decision easy. She'd call Mia and tell her to pick someone else.

But Della was so adamant that Luci not give anything up or screw up her own life, that it made the dilemma even more vexing. It felt like Luci was bound to disappoint her either way she chose.

As she turned a corner on her favorite wooded path in Dalesville, she laid her eyes on a dirt trail that extended off the paved path, one that she had run often during her youth. The trail was originally intended for horseback riding, but in recent years, runners and bicyclists were much more likely to be seen than any sort of farm animal.

She paused for a moment before stepping onto the trail. It was getting a bit dark now, and Luci felt a bit uneasy. In all her years of running it, she'd never run the trail alone. Not after Georgia Keats.

Georgia was a Dalesville native, who was about ten years older than Della and Luci. She'd gone running on the same trail years earlier, when Luci and Della were in first grade, and never returned. Her body was found three months later in the creek bed that ran parallel to the trail during a drought. Her parents had never had a funeral, so no one but them had seen the body. As rumors usually do in small towns, stories spread like wildfire that the authorities were lying about recovering her body.

Tall tales claimed that Georgia's body was still lost in the woods, only to be found when the rains were scarce. It became a morbid obsession of Dalesville youth for a while, and for years after, teens made it their personal business to head into the woods after a few beers, searching for poor old Georgia. Usually, the most exciting happenings in Dalesville revolved around a sale at the supermarket, or a new tractor on display during the Dalesville Day parade. So, naturally, Georgia's death shook the whole town. The Keatses eventually moved out of the state, unable to cope with the constant whispering and speculation.

Despite that dark memory, the trail had remained a favorite running spot for Luci and Dayton. It was where they, and Della and Jackson, had spent many of their teenage nights, flirting with the darkness.

And it had also been the place where she lost her virginity to Dayton when she was seventeen.

Just before dark, they'd taken a big blanket with them until they reached the big clearing a few miles in. She shook her head to clear away the memory, took a breath, and took off. The deeper into the woods she got, the clearer she hoped her head would be.

But she realized about a mile down the trail that she was wrong. She felt even shittier than before she left, and the deep purple sky above was unrelenting, making it hard to see down the path. As she squinted ahead in the last light of dusk, she made out the silhouette of another runner headed her way.

Another uneasy feeling spun through her stomach. She pivoted to turn back, but as she did, she felt the tip of her shoe slip under a risen tree root. She had committed too much momentum to the next step, and before she knew it, she was flying forward. She braced for impact, quickly putting her palms out to take the brunt of it. She hit the ground hard, skating across the rocks and leaves in front of her, skidding to an ultra-graceful stop in the dirt.

Her hands stung immediately, and she could feel blood trickling down her knees. Before she could push herself to stand, she felt two large hands wrapping around her biceps, pulling her to her feet. She knelt over, putting her hands on her knees to catch her breath and slow her heart rate down.

"Thank you," she managed to get out between her long, drawn-out breaths. She was pretty sure she saw her life flash before her eyes.

"Are you okay?" she heard him ask, and suddenly, the pain wasn't in her new wounds anymore.

"Jesus Christ, Dayton. Are you going to show up *everywhere* I go while I'm here?" she asked, dusting the loose dirt and leaves from her legs.

"Sorry. I run this trail almost every night," he said, matter-of-factly, reminding her that *she* was the one who left. "Are you alright?"

"I'm fine," she said, examining her hands before she started walking. Her knees stung too bad to run just yet. She was sure she'd be bruised like a peach the next morning. But aside from that pain, it hurt even more that he saw her fall.

She had been determined since she came back for him to only see her in positions of power, grace, traits she never really had to possess while she was with him. She needed him to see that he wasn't the end of her. But now he was following closely behind as she walked, and she felt her weaker side slipping into dangerous nostalgia for a moment. The last time she'd been here with him, way back in high school, they'd been making. . . uh, memories.

"You can keep going. I'm fine," she said again, crossing her arms over her chest.

"No, I'd rather walk with you, if that's okay," he said. She sighed loudly. She probably should have told him to keep going, to leave her alone, but she decided to trade pride for safety until she was out of the woods.

They walked in complete silence the entire way down the trail until they reached the paved path, him two steps behind her the whole way.

"Luci," he finally said, the second they reached the pavement again, "I really want to talk to you."

Ha. This whole game was getting a little old. A year ago, shit, even just six months ago, she'd be dying to know what he had to say. She'd been *falling apart* trying to figure out what could have been worth him leaving her the way he did. Breaking her like he had, never once checking in to see if she had survived. It had been a long three years without him, and some of her wounds still felt fresh, no matter how many miles she put between them.

And that hadn't really changed. She wanted to know so badly why he had ended things. But she was too afraid to hear it. If it wasn't a good enough reason, she'd be angry, hurt, broken all over again. And if it *was* a legitimate reason, then she just might have to forgive him. And if she didn't hate him anymore, then she just might love him. And that was the scariest scenario of all.

"Dayton, you have nothing to say that I want to hear," she said, never taking her eyes off of the path in front of her.

"Luci—"

"No, Dayton. Just stop," she said. He sighed, running his hand through his delicious sandy locks. He wore a t-shirt with the sleeves cut off and long basketball shorts, and he looked like a model for a Nike ad. But she couldn't let herself linger too long.

"Can I at least help you with those?" he asked, pointing to her hands. "I have a first aid kit in my car."

She pictured it, her sitting in the back seat of his cop car, legs dangling out of the back seat while he dabbed her hands, gently wrapping them in gauze. She'd flinch when he hit a sore spot, and he'd gently caress them, bringing them to his lips to cure them with his magic kiss. Then her arms would slowly wrap around his neck, her fingers running through his hair. His arms would slide around her waist, and her legs would wrap around his. . .

Not today, Mr. Officer.

"No," she said. "You had five years to take care of me, to be there for me, like I always tried to be for you. You had three years *between* then and now to pick up the damn phone and explain yourself. Or write me another one of your useless letters. And you didn't. So no, Dayton. You can't 'help me with these.' You don't get to be my hero, anymore."

With that, she pushed off of her toes and into a run, the fastest pace she'd gone all day, despite the searing pain from her knees and shins.

She didn't stop till she got back to Della's door, panting and crying, fighting desperately not to hyperventilate as the lump in her throat threatened to stop all breathing.

# ELEVEN
*Della*

Della heard the front door open and slam just after she shoveled a huge spoonful of Rocky Road into her mouth.

Luci made a b-line to the sink, turning on the faucet and making a hissing sound with her teeth as the water hit her bloody palms.

"What the hell happened?" Della said, walking toward her and immediately reaching in the cabinet above the sink for a box of Band-Aids.

"I fell on a freakin' tree root," Luci said, gently scrubbing at the dirt that was stuck to her scrapes.

"Here, sit down," Della said, pulling out one of the kitchen chairs and running a cloth under warm water. With as much urgency as her growing body could muster, she grabbed the bottle of peroxide from the hall bathroom and shuffled back to Luci, who winced as Della poured it over her knees and hands, letting it bubble before gently dabbing it.

"He was there," Luci said, wiping her dripping

nose on her sleeve.

"Who?"

"Dayton," Luci said.

"He was where? In the woods?" Della asked, pushing herself back up to her feet from her kneeling position. Luci nodded. "Why? Did you go together?" Della asked. She had hoped the answer would be yes, but judging by the tears, she knew it wasn't.

"No, of course not. He happened to be there. Of course he was right there when I fell. Tried to be the hero. And he won't leave me alone about talking about things," she said.

"Oh," Della said. She didn't want to push, but she really did want Luci to have some closure, some peace with everything that had happened. And, though she'd never admit it to Luci, Della wanted Dayton to have some peace of his own, too. It had become clear to her over the past few weeks that the way things ended was still eating him alive every day. And he'd been such a friend to her since Jackson passed, and such a friend to Jackson when he was still alive. Well, when she and Jackson *let* him be. She wanted that peace for him, too.

"And what do you want to do about it?"

"Nothing. I really don't. I don't need to know. I just need him to leave me be," Luci said, standing up and examining her newly patched hands and knees. Della couldn't help but think she looked like a toddler learning to ride a bike.

And that reminded her that someday, her toddler would need to learn to ride a bike. And she'd have to be the one to teach him, all alone.

She nodded to Luci, re-entering the conversation and leaving behind the distraction of her own grief.

"I understand," she said. "Listen. I've been thinking about what you said, about Cora. And what I would have wanted Jackson to do. And you're right. How about I make you a deal? I'll read the letter, and maybe sit down with Cora, if you think about doing the same with Dayton."

Luci thought for a second, biting her lip as she looked at Della. Finally, she gave a reluctant nod.

"Okay," she said. Della smiled.

"I was about to go plop down in my bed and eat the rest of this Rocky Road. Care to join?" Now Luci smiled.

"Just ran five miles, but yes, let's make up for those burnt calories," she said, reaching for a spoon in the silverware drawer and following Della up the steps.

Della squinted in the dim light of the television, pushing herself to her feet for what felt like the hundredth time that night. This baby seemed to have made its home in the dead center of her bladder, and was now doing what she could only assume was a fully-choreographed gymnastics routine on it.

As she walked drearily toward the bathroom, she turned to see Luci perched up on the pillows, fast asleep, spoon still in her bandaged hand. Della slipped the spoon out of her fingers and pulled the covers up around her. Della had enjoyed taking care of her friend tonight, despite the pain, both physically and emotionally, that she knew Luci was in. For the first time in a few weeks, she didn't feel like a complete invalid, useless to those around her.

And, she was reminded that she was capable of taking care of other humans. And that she loved doing it. And that that was the reason she couldn't wait to be a mother in the first place. The thought made her smile and cradle her belly in her hands as she walked into the bathroom, flipping on the light and shutting the door.

As she washed her hands and dried them, she noticed her scale peeking out from behind the vanity.

She was weighed at every appointment, but she didn't dare ask, and the techs at the office wouldn't dare tell her. But for some reason, at 2:29 in the morning, she had to know how much she had gained. She nudged the scale out from behind the vanity with her toe until it sat flush against the back wall. She took a deep breath and stepped on. She looked down, only to see her belly. She giggled to herself as she knelt further and further over, steadying herself, until she could just make out the numbers. Her eyes widened. She leapt off the scale, stripping down to nothing but her underwear. Surely her pajamas weighed twenty pounds.

When she got back on, the number changed by only a quarter of a pound, and she slipped off the scale again, defeated. As she used her toes to lift her pants up to her hand, she paused at the sight of herself in the mirror. Her eyes widened as she saw them, creeping down her sides and hips, carving their trails down her thighs. She let out a blood-curdling yelp.

Luci stumbled into the bathroom groggily, rubbing her eyes.

"What? What?" she asked.

Della just stood there, virtually naked, staring at herself in the mirror.

"Look," she said, pointing a shaky finger to the dark red stretch marks that seemed to be taking over the lower half of her body. "They're *everywhere!*" she cried.

Luci looked them over, then looked up at Della, as if to gauge just how serious of a crisis this actually was.

Then Della looked back at her, realizing how dramatic she had just been.

Then the two of them doubled over in laughter.

"They are awesome, Della," Luci finally said after she collected herself. "You're earning your stripes."

Della sighed and smiled as she looked them over one last time. Jackson would have said something exactly like that.

"Well, I suppose it doesn't matter anyways," she said, pulling her pajama pants back on. "I don't need to impress anyone with silky smooth, stripe-free thighs no more! I'm embracing my mom-bod, and I plan to die an old maid."

"Oh, would you stop it?" Luci said, brushing her off. "You are going to be a MILF, whether you want to believe it or not. Now, go back to sleep before your next bathroom visit."

◊

A few days later, it was already time for Della's twenty-eight week appointment. And although the last one was a little emotional, she was looking forward to this one. With the thought of putting the nursery together and her long-lost maternal instincts somewhat restored, she was ready. Plus, it was time for another sonogram, and nothing quite took her breath away like the sight of her tiny little sidekick rolling around inside of her.

"Okay, go ahead and lay back," the sonographer said. She was short and stout, with cherry-red cheeks that reminded Della of Mrs. Claus. Della breathed heavily as she stared at the screen, squinting.

"Tell me the truth, is that really my baby, or do you guys just have a screensaver of some wavy black lines that you put on for everyone?" Della asked. Luci snorted behind her. But the usually cheery sonographer didn't laugh. She didn't even crack a smile.

"Hmm," she said, turning the machine off and wiping the end of her magic wand.

"Hmm? Is something wrong?" Della asked, pushing herself up on her elbows. Luci took a step forward.

"Your doctor will have to discuss it with you. Unfortunately, I'm not at liberty to discuss it." She waited until the images were printed, tearing the bottom one off and handing the rest of the strip to Della. "She should be in in just a few minutes," the sonographer said, walking out.

Della's eyes grew wide as she stared down at the strip of images. There was a perfect profile shot of her little man, and one where his feet were outstretched as if he were kicking a ball. She counted his toes desperately, only to find that there were, in fact, ten. She tried to figure out what else might be wrong with her perfect baby boy.

All of her first trimester tests had come back normal. She'd taken all of her vitamins. She'd done everything she read about in her baby books, and followed every tip from her pregnancy app.

"I'm sure it's nothing," Luci said, reading her mind and squeezing her hand.

After a short eternity, Dr. Malloy finally knocked on the door.

"Come in," Della said, pulling the paper covering up around her tighter.

"How are we feeling today?" Dr. Malloy asked, situating herself on the rolling stool across from Della. She was a tall thin woman, with her dark brown skin radiant under the fluorescent office lights. Under her lab coat, she wore a beautiful green dress, tied tight around her tiny waist. Della wasn't sure if it was just that extra weight she was currently packing skewing her view, but it seemed like everyone around her was shrinking as she was doubling in size.

"A little nervous, now. Is something wrong with

the baby?" Della asked.

"The baby has what we call a choroid plexus cyst on his brain," Dr. Malloy said. Della felt her heart rate increase instantly.

"Okay. . . what exactly is that?"

"So, if you look here," Dr. Malloy said, scooting closer and showing Della the close-up image of the baby's head—the one that that sonographer had taken with her— "it's right here, on the right side of his brain. It happens in about one to two percent of babies."

"So, is it serious? Will he be okay?" Della asked. Luci squeezed her arm, but she barely noticed.

"He should be just fine. These typically develop in utero like this, and then dissolve before the baby is even born. We will continue to monitor him; you will receive a sonogram at every appointment going forward until it is gone," Dr. Malloy said, with a smile on her face all the while.

"And what happens if it doesn't dissolve?" Luci asked, knowing Della was afraid to.

"Well, let's just worry about that when the time comes. For now, we will just keep an eye. Otherwise, his growth and heart rate look wonderful. Looks like you have a very healthy baby growing in there," Dr. Malloy said, standing up to shake both of their hands. "We will see you in a few weeks."

Della was silent on the way home. She hadn't taken her hands off of her stomach since they had left the office. She'd been so cautious throughout her entire pregnancy. She'd stayed away from deli meat, hadn't gotten her hair dyed since she found out she was pregnant. She'd been drinking lots of water, getting lots of rest. And her freaking husband died. Did she really deserve this? Why was this happening?

"It's going to be okay, Della Bee," Luci said as she pulled up in front of the tiny bungalow. Della looked out at her perfect little house. The house she and Jackson fell in love with before they even got out of their realtor's car. The house where Jackson had shouted "let's get it, baby!" before they had even crossed the threshold. God, she missed him.

"Dell? You okay?" Luci asked, waiting for her to get out of the car.

"What if I lose him, too?" Della asked, choking back tears. The sound of a weed whacker coming from behind the house startled them both, Della jumping to wipe her cheeks. She would be okay. She was always okay.

And the baby would be okay. He had to be. She couldn't do this again.

# TWELVE
*Luci*

Luci wanted to concentrate on Della and the cyst currently growing on her unborn child's brain. She wanted to be there for her, fully invested and focused on the problem at hand, and figure out how to make Della feel better. But she couldn't. Because Dayton was busy, whacking the weeds next to the Della's house. Shirtless. With his stupid, sexy, chiseled, sweaty body, clenched everywhere, shaping up the lawn like a Goddamn professional.

"Dayton!" Della called, instantly forcing pep into her step as she walked across the front lawn toward him. "What are you doing here? You don't have to do all this!" she cried, laying a kiss on his cheek.

"I talked to Cash at the reception, and he mentioned he had to head back to school. I just thought it might be helpful," he said, shrugging the weedwacker in the air.

"I know how to mow the damn lawn, you know," Luci said, appearing behind Della. Della shot her a look.

"This is so sweet of you, Dayton. I really, really appreciate it. Can I pay you?" she asked. Dayton looked offended. He shook his head. "Okay. How about a home-cooked meal?"

"*That* I will take," he said with his killer smile. The same smile that had gotten Luci to do some unmentionable things back in the day. Things she'd rather not think about while she was trying to hate him. Things she shouldn't think about given that she couldn't just hop in a cold shower at any moment. *Whoo,* the sun was suddenly feeling *hot.*

"I'm going to start some dinner now. Should be ready in about twenty minutes. Come on in when you're done!" Della called, using the railing to pull herself up the front steps.

"Really? You have to invite him *in?* Are you trying to kill me?" Luci asked once they were inside.

"You are awfully dramatic," Della said, laying her things down on the kitchen table and opening up the fridge. Luci would have liked to rag on her more for it, but Della was actually in a good mood. She was distracted, and that was all that mattered. No damn choroid plexus cysts to worry about right now. This pregnancy thing sure was getting her off the hook. Luci would have to remember this all once the baby was born.

"Fine. I'm going out back to work. I'll eat when you and your new best friend are done."

Luci grabbed her laptop, her phone, and unbeknownst to Della, the torn off image of the baby's brain, with the cyst circled in bright red ink. She headed out onto the patio, which Jackson had originally planned to be an outdoor mancave. But, too much HGTV and one-too-many visits to HomeGoods , and *boom*, Della had transformed it into a backyard oasis that looked to be designed by the Property Brothers themselves. It was cozy, with the dark wicker furniture all pointed toward the fire pit.  It faced a huge open field behind their neighborhood, one of the selling points for Jackson and Della when they bought the house.

Luci tried to imagine what their planned life might have looked like in this sweet little house. But the image of Jackson running down the path with a miniature version of himself on his shoulders was washed away by the deafening sound of the weed whacker on the other side. Stupid Dayton.

She opened her laptop and turned it on, then looked back toward the house, as if Della might be spying on her through the window. When she was sure she was in the clear, she pulled the image out again, staring down at it.

Tomorrow was one month. Tomorrow, she had to give Mia her answer. She had to either claim her rightful place as heir to the Vice President's office, or pass on quite possibly the best professional opportunity that might ever come her way. But as she stared down at the tiny cyst, she knew exactly what her answer would be.

"Hey," she heard him say, just as she was sinking back into the plush cushions. She sat immediately back up.

"Aren't you supposed to be inside?" Luci asked, tucking the picture under her computer. He was shirted up now, but his muscles still beamed through the thin fabric.

"Della's not quite done with dinner yet, so she sent me out here," he said, throwing back what was left in the cup of lemonade that Della had so *sweetly* made him. Damnit, Della. Whose side was she on, anyway?

"Of course she did," Luci said, pulling the laptop

closer to her and typing away so frivolously, that she knew he could tell it was all for show.

"So, what's eatin' at you?" he asked, taking a seat in the chair adjacent to her. She pulled her legs in closer to her body.

"Excuse me?"

"Something's bothering you," he said, matter-of-factly, chewing away at a piece of ice from his glass.

"You mean, besides you?" she asked. He cracked a half-version of his killer smile, and she felt her stomach do a flip.

"Yes," he chuckled, "besides me."

She wanted to curse him out, tell him to leave her alone, to go back inside and be with Della. But the fact that he could still be with her for less than thirty seconds and know that something wasn't right, to know that she was hurting, made her pull back on her guns a bit. To be honest, she hadn't been able to get much off her chest since she got back to Dalesville. Of course, she could vent all day and night about Dayton to Della. But she couldn't vent about *Della* to Della. She sighed, putting the computer back down on the table and picking up the sonogram picture. She handed it to him.

"What's this?" he asked.

"That's the baby's brain," she said, pointing to it. "And *that* is the cyst that's currently growing on it."

Dayton's eyes widened as he looked up at her, the concern in them *almost* endearing.

"What does this mean? Will the baby be okay?" he asked. Luci shrugged.

"They want to check on it for the next few appointments to make sure it's shrinking. It should hopefully be totally gone before he's even born," she told him, leaning back in her seat, a little more at ease, now that the conversation wasn't about the two of them.

"Oh man, poor Della. How's she doing?" he asked.

"She's worried, understandably. I mean, the doctor didn't seem too concerned, but this is her child we're talking about. Of course she's a nervous wreck," she said.

"Right. And I imagine with Jackson. . . I imagine it's just harder for her without that support system. Although, I know she has a great one in you," he said, nodding toward her. The faintest smile crawled across her lips, then disappeared with the wind.

"What is it?" he asked. Damn, he was good.

"It's just that the timing is impeccable," she said with a sardonic laugh.

"How do you mean?"

"Well, tomorrow I'm supposed to call my boss and let her know whether or not I accept the VP position at Millerston. But today was pretty much the answer I needed."

"Oh yeah? And what answer was that?" he asked, looking straight into her eyes.

"That I can't go back," she said, twirling the sonogram picture around in her fingers. "How could I? How could I leave her, I mean, in general, but now, after this stupid thing decided to park itself on *our* baby's brain? How can I get back on a plane and fly thousands of miles away, not knowing if she, or the baby for that matter, will be alright?" she asked.

To Luci's surprise, she felt that knot forming in her throat again, and the tears welling in her eyes. She composed herself, doing a series of deep breaths. She would *not* cry in front of him.

"Wow, Luce, that's a lot for you to handle," he said. She scoffed.

"You know, every time I go to feel sorry for myself, I remember that she's a *widow.* A *pregnant* widow. She's lost her everything. It feels so selfish to even *think* about complaining," Luci said, her voice just above a whisper.

Dayton leaned in close, and she could smell the gas from the mower, the grass from the lawn, the scent of him—so familiar, so delicious, that she consciously had to stop herself from licking her lips.

"First of all," he said, "you're allowed to have struggles, too. You don't have to compare your situation to hers. You're allowed to hurt, too."

Ha. She knew that. From three years of experience. He went on.

"And secondly, if that job is what you want, just know that Della will be taken care of. I promise you that I'll be here for her. And that baby. I owe that to Jackson. And to you. I want you to be happy, Luci. I will do whatever she needs here, if that means you can have what you want most."

Now the tears were making their way toward the front of her eyes. She looked down, and slowly slid her hand out from his. No way, mister. You keep your hands and your sweetness and your sweatiness to yourself. She shook her head.

"She needs me. And I *want* to be here for them. I can't miss this," Luci said, looking down at that evil cyst one more time. Dayton sat back in his chair and nodded.

"In that case, I'll be here for you, too," he said. As she was about to protest, Della opened the back door.

"It's ready, you two," she said. "Come on in!"

"I'll be in in one minute," Luci said, "I just have to make one phone call."

# THIRTEEN
*Della*

To Della's pleasant surprise, dinner was actually not awkward. Although, ever since she heard Luci quitting her job out on her back patio, she couldn't exactly focus one-hundred percent. But that conversation had to wait until Dayton left.

"So, Dayton, how's your mother doing?" Della asked, taking a sip of her iced tea and looking from Luci to Dayton.

"She's doing okay," he said. "Still working at the thrift shop up town." Della nodded. Mrs. Briggs was always quiet, kept to herself. The rest of the gang didn't really know her. But she had to have done something right, seeing as how Dayton turned out. She'd raised him all by herself, with nothing but an uncle a few hours away. But Dayton was always extremely close with her, something that Della and Luci had always found endearing.

"How is your mom, Luci?" Dayton asked, cutting up the parmesan-encrusted chicken breast on his plate.

"She's fine," Luci said, never looking up from her plate. Della knew that she planned to end their conversing there. But that was fine. If Luci didn't want to give him the details on her life, Della could certainly do it for her.

"She goes out to Seattle a few times to see her every year. She's loving the retired life," Della said. "And she has just been marvelous through this whole thing. Honestly, I don't know where I'd be without her. Or her cooking!"

Dayton smiled.

"Well, your cooking is amazing, too, Della. That baby is going to be one well-fed kid," he said, pointing his fork toward her bump. She smiled and instinctively put a hand on it.

"So, I heard you two had a run-in on the path the other day," Della said. She felt like stirring up some trouble tonight for two reasons: one, because she was pregnant, and therefore, fragile. Luci couldn't retaliate for another few months. And two, because this whole cat-and-mouse game was taking entirely too long for Della's liking. She either needed it to go somewhere, or be completely squashed. Get on with it, people.

She decided to ignore the hole Luci's gaze was burning through her and lean in toward Dayton sweetly across the table.

"Uh, yeah, we did. How are your hands, by the way, Luci?" he asked.

"Fine," she said again.

Oh no, this was not going to be it, Della thought. She shot a foot out toward Luci's shin, making her jump. Luci glared back at Della, but finally gave in. She sighed.

"They are pretty much all healed up," Luci said, holding out her palms.

"I think it's funny," Della said, a devious smile creeping across her face, "that you two happened to bump into each other on the same path where you bumped uglies all those years ago."

Now Luci looked like someone had slapped her in the face. Both she and Dayton stared at Della wide-eyed. Dayton pounded his fist against his chest, coughing up whatever he had been chewing on. He took a huge gulp of his lemonade.

Suddenly, Luci burst into a fit of laughter, doubling over across the table with Della following her lead. Dayton soon followed suit, shaking his head, his cheeks blushing with embarrassment.

"You are the *worst,*" Luci said when she caught her breath. "You're so—"

"I know, I know. I'm *so* lucky I'm pregnant," she said. "And I plan to continue using that superpower until this kid is expelled from my body."

"Well, on that note," Dayton said, putting his napkin over his plate as if to surrender, "that was amazing. I should probably get going, though. I have to get to work in a few hours."

Della started to stand, but he waved her back down. "Don't get up, don't get up. Thank you for everything," he said, kneeling down to kiss her forehead. "It was amazing. I'll come back in a week to mow again."

She nodded and smiled.

"Thank you so much, Dayton. I'll have dinner waiting for you next week. Luci will walk you out," she said, leaning back in her chair as if she were some sort of criminal mastermind. Luci glared at her again, and Della gave her nothing in return but a raised eyebrow. Luci rolled her eyes and pushed herself up from the table, leading him out to the porch. Della watched through the window as they spoke for a moment, before Dayton started down the front steps. If Della wasn't mistaken, that was a smile creeping onto Luci's face, but of course, it had magically disappeared as she came inside.

"I'm so glad *that's* over," Luci said, collecting the dishes from the table and bringing them to the sink.

"Oh, I know, it must have been *so painful* to sit with your smokin' hot ex-boyfriend who is still into you," Della said, reaching up on her tip-toes to the top shelf of the cupboard where Jackson had stashed the Tupperware.

Jackson.

"If you put it up there, I won't be able to reach it!" she had told him as he was neatly stacking every container they owned on the top shelf.

"Guess you'll have to keep me around, then," he had said, wrapping his arms around her waist and kissing her cheek. "Otherwise, you'll never be able to save leftovers *ever* again."

A painful smile came over her face as the memory quickly faded.

"Oh, shut up," Luci said. "But I did agree to have dinner with him tomorrow night." Luci paused for a second, lifting her eyes to Della, waiting for her reaction.

"*Finally!*" she shouted, lifting her hands up and doing some sort of pregnant twerk.

"Oh my god, you're insane," Luci said, with a giggle.

"Hey, give me a break," Della said. "I haven't seen my own vagina in weeks now. So *excuse me* for living vicariously through yours."

Luci paused to laugh again before putting the last of the leftovers into the containers and piling them up in the fridge.

"I'm not sure what you think is going to happen, but I promise that *this* hoo-ha is on lockdown forever when it comes to him."

Della rolled her eyes.

"Oh, please. You let him get in your pants at your aunt's *wedding*. There is nothing stopping you when he whips out the magic stick," she said.

Luci laughed again, shaking her head as she put the last of the dishes in the dishwasher.

"So," Della said, figuring now was as good of a time as any, "are we going to talk about how you quit your job tonight?"

Della watched as Luci's body grew stiff, shoulders hunched slightly in defense. Della sat back down at the table and pulled out the chair next to her, patting it. Luci sighed and sat down.

"Did he tell you?"

"Nope. But there's a small crack in the back door that Jackson never got around to fixing. Guess it's not so soundproof."

Luci nodded and looked down at her folded hands on the table.

"Luci, how could you do that? I *told* you. . ." Della started to say, shaking her head.

"I know what you said," Luci said, "but there's just no way I'm leaving you, or him, right now." She reached out and put a hand on the bump. Now, Della felt the tears prickling at her eyes. Damn these pregnancy hormones.

"Luci, this isn't right. You're supposed to be that girl, you know? You're supposed to be that girl that women show to their daughters and say: 'look at her! She did it all on her own, and so can you!' You're supposed to be *that* girl. I mean, don't get me wrong, I am thrilled to have you here. You've been absolutely amazing. But I can't let you go through with this. I mean, you don't even know if you want kids at all. If you stay here with me, well, there is a one-hundred-percent chance that you're getting one in your life. They say most pregnancies result in a baby, you know."

Luci smiled and reached out for Della's hands.

"Della, there will be other jobs. There will be other companies, there will be other positions. This arrangement is perfect for right now. Mia is letting me keep my current job till the end of the year, working from home. So I can keep my job and stay here with you. She'll put feelers out for me if I'm ever back on the West Coast. But right now, I need to be here with you. And my baby. Please, don't feel guilty about this. This is my decision. If the tables were turned, I know your ass would be right next to mine. Am I right?" she asked.

Della nodded. Luci had a point. She would have done exactly the same thing if Luci had lost her everything.

Although, Luci sort of did. And Della didn't do as much as she probably should have. She let Luci take off, leaving all the painful memories behind. And in the last three years, she'd only been out to Seattle one time.

It was like Luci could read her mind.

"Della, please stop worrying. I am going to be just fine. I will find another job. You are only going to have this baby once."

Della nodded.

"You know, people are going to start thinking we're a lesbian couple," she said. Luci laughed.

"They might as well. You're the damn love of my life, Della Bee."

Della didn't even realize the tears were falling until Luci reached out to wipe one away.

"Well," Della said, composing herself, "we have to go shopping."

"For what?"

"For something skimpy, yet, not *too* skimpy, for your date tomorrow."

"Oh. My. *God.* It is *not* a date," Luci insisted,

crossing her arms.

"Okay, fine. But you can still have hot hate-sex on a not-date. So we still need to go."

Luci rolled her eyes again, but it didn't stop her from grabbing her purse off the counter and following Della out the front door.

As they strolled the aisles of women's evening wear, Luci shot down most of Della's picks.

"Too much boob," she said to the low-cut black dress that Della grabbed.

"Way too short," she said to the red mini-skirt Della plucked off another rack.

"Okay, Miss I-Have-Something-To-Say-About-Everything, what do you have to say about this one?" Della asked, nodding to Luci's reflection in the mirror in front of them. It was a teal halter dress that was tight to the waist, then flowed out a bit. The back was open, and of course, as usual, it fit perfectly on Luci's perfect figure.

"This one. . . " Luci said, her voice trailing off a bit as she admired her derriere in the mirror, "this one might just work."

"Phew, *finally*," Della said, pushing herself up from the extra-low fitting room bench. She watched as Luci pulled her shirt back over her head, and something in her expression changed. "What's up?"

"I'm just. . . I don't know. I guess I'm just nervous," Luci said.

Della nodded. She'd been making light of the situation between Luci and Dayton for weeks now, but the truth was, her friend was still hurting. And as sweet and charming as Dayton may be, he had still broken her, leaving her with not so much as a reason why.

"I know, Luce, I know. But regardless of what happens, I really think this will be good. Honestly. You might get some answers. Some freaking closure. And if nothing else, you'll get that hate-sex we've been talking about and high-tail it outta there," she said.

Luci laughed, nudging her gently.

"Hey," Della said, nudging her back, "seriously. It's all going to be okay."

They walked down the aisles, Della poking around in the maternity section a bit, still not fully admitting to herself that she was *that* big.

"Hey," Luci said, lifting up on the sleeve of a green sweater on one of the racks, "I forgot about our deal."

"What deal?" Della asked, knowing exactly what deal Luci was talking about.

"Our Cora and Dayton deal. I'm meeting with Dayton. You have to meet with Cora."

Della sighed.

"Fine. I'll think about it," she said.

As they made their way toward the front of the store, something stopped Della in her tracks.

A tiny little t-shirt, baby blue in color, that read "mom's #1 guy," in big, white block letters. She reached out and grabbed the sleeve, running her fingers down the tiny seams. She smiled.

"I guess I need to get me some of these soon, huh?" she asked.

◊

That evening, Luci and Della called it a night shortly after they got back from the store. Della stared at herself in the mirror as she brushed her teeth, lifting her shirt on and off of her bump, admiring her profile, checking to see if she could magically view her feet again weeks after they disappeared beneath her massive middle.

As she made her way back into the bedroom, she paused as she felt a foot to her rib cage. She smiled, bringing her hand to it.

"Hi, baby boy," she whispered, rubbing it. She pulled the covers down on Jackson's side of the bed, setting her phone down on his nightstand. Then she took a breath, and slowly pulled out the drawer.

Inside, sat an envelope with "Mrs. Niles" on the front in perfect cursive.

She took another breath before running her finger along the seam and tearing it open.

*Dear Mrs. Niles,*

*I've been trying to write this letter since the night it all happened, but to be honest, I wasn't sure what to say.*

*There are a few things I want to say, and I don't think I could do it all in person. The first, is that I'm so, so sorry. I can't get past the fact that Mr. Niles won't ever step foot in your home again. That he won't smile at you, or meet your child.*

*I wish, more than anything, that I hadn't taken a drink of my soda when I came back from the restroom. I know better. . .always get a new one. I wish Mr. Niles wasn't the one who saw us in the parking lot. I wish I had the strength to fight him off myself.*

*The second is that I'm grateful. I don't know why Mr. Niles was in that lot at the same time as me, but I like to think of him as some sort of guardian angel. I can never repay him, or you, for the sacrifices he made, but it's because of him that I'm alive to write this letter right now.*

*The last thing I want to say is that if you are comfortable with it, I'd like to keep in touch. I'd like to be there for anything you or your child may need. I'd like a chance to get to know you, and get to know the man that Mr. Niles was.*

*I understand that the wounds are still fresh—believe me, I get it. But if you are ever in a place where you think you might be able to handle it, I would love to talk with you.*

*And if you never get to that point, I will completely understand.*

*I am forever grateful to you and your family, Mrs. Niles.*

*Sincerely,*

*Cora Lowes*
*555-4030*

Della sniffed as she wiped her tears across the back of her arm.

# FOURTEEN
*Luci*

The next night, Luci was ready for her dinner out twenty-five minutes before Dayton was supposed pick her up. She sat on Della's couch and pretended to be relaxed, casually flipping through channels with her shoes off and her feet up. But her hair was done, her makeup was perfect, and she was wearing her best push-up bra.

The last time she was sitting around waiting for him, he never showed. So she'd be damned if she was going to be caught doing that again. If he never came, she'd be perfectly content here on the couch, watching *Family Feud*. This dress? She wore this kind of thing around the house all the time.

But to her pleasant surprise, Dayton arrived and knocked on the door early. Five minutes early, to be exact. Della sprung from the recliner, as fast as one carrying around thirty extra pounds can spring, to answer it. She greeted Dayton with a hug.

"Well, don't you look nice," she said, patting his chest.

"Well, thank you," he said. He was dressed in a steel gray button-down that matched his eyes, and dark jeans. His sleeves were rolled halfway, just enough so that the bottom of the sleeve tattoo on his right arm showed. He must have just gotten his hair trimmed; it was shaped neatly, but his face had a little stubble, which was just the way Luci had preferred it. Whenever they'd kiss, she'd rub her chin against his and tell him how sexy his five-o'clock shadow was. She wondered if he remembered this, or if it was just a coincidence that he hadn't shaved today.

"Wow," he said as she made her way to the door. She smiled, feeling the fire rise in her cheeks.

"You two kids have fun," Della said, "but don't keep her out too late." Dayton smiled and nodded.

"No problem, ma'am," he said, tipping an imaginary hat.

Just as Luci stepped out onto the porch, Della grabbed her hand.

"Luci?" she whispered.

"Yes?"

"If you do think you're going to be out late, can you just text me and let me know? I worry more than I used to," Della said, her eyes falling to the ground. Luci cocked her head with sympathy.

"Of course," she answered, squeezing Della's hand. "I'm sure I won't be too late anyways. But I'll let you know where I am."

"Thank you."

As they made their way down the steps, Dayton stepped in front of her, opening the passenger door like a perfect gentleman. He had traded in his old pickup truck for a nice new Chevy Tahoe, and it suited him.

"You look amazing," he said, getting in.

"Thanks. You clean up better than I remember," she said with a smile. "So, where are we going?"

"Well, if it's alright with you, I thought we could just go back to my place. I don't really see this conversation going over well in public. Plus, I thought I could cook for you. I bought Spongebob mac and cheese," he said.

She couldn't stop herself from smiling if she wanted to. As a teenager, she had had the pallet of a six-year-old, and Dayton and her friends never let her forget it. But she did *love* a good bowl of Spongebob mac and cheese. She didn't care what anyone said, it tasted better when it was in the shape of cartoon characters than when it was regular noodles.

"Let's do it," she said. The mac and cheese sounded great, but having to have the conversation in private totally freaked her out. What in the world was he going to tell her? Oh, God. What if there was someone else? It was probably Joanna. Or what if he found out he had some love child somewhere? That would be pretty hard to do, considering he'd only slept with one other person (you guessed it: Joanna), and it was a year before he dated Luci. She sat quiet in the passenger seat as they made their way through town, to the very last few miles of the Dalesville line.

She smiled as he pulled down a long driveway toward a small farmhouse, one that she had pointed out to him a million times when they were teens.

"You bought this place?" she asked.

"I did. Mr. Treefield sold it after his wife passed about a year ago. It was in pretty bad shape. But I'm fixing it up slowly, when I have the time," he said. She nodded.

The house was built in the late 1800s, and it showed. Its white paint was chipped in multiple places, and a few of the dark green shutters appeared to be hanging by a thread. But she could tell that Dayton had fixed up the bowed wood of the front porch, and given the front door a fresh coat of paint. It sat on thirty or so acres of green grass, mowed into perfectly straight and even lines. Originally, the farm had been over three hundred acres, but the Treefields had sold piece by piece to various builders and developers over the years when it became too hard to manage.

"It looks great," she said, following him up onto the porch.

"It's getting there," he said, holding open the screen door. Inside, the house smelled like seasoned wood, and she instantly felt herself relax, despite the growing anticipation. She made a mental note of all the doors, in case things went south and she needed to make a fast exit.

"So, one bowl, or two?" he asked, pointing to the table for her to take a seat.

"One, to start," she said, "I don't want to get too crazy."

To her pleasant surprise, the conversation carried on fairly seamlessly. She asked him about work, and she learned that he had volunteered to take the early morning shift for a while so that one of the other guys could be home with his new baby during the nights.

The week before, he'd had to arrest Cory Blake, the younger, devious brother of one of their high school classmates, Courtney Blake, for stealing three cartons of cigarettes from the 7-11 in town.

And a few weeks before that, he'd had to deliver the news to the parents of a seventeen-year-old kid upcounty that their son had been killed in a crash when he was texting and driving.

"That one was tough," he said. "But so far, the toughest of them all has been Jackson." Her eyes found his, and to her surprise, her hand found his, too.

"What exactly happened that night?" she asked,

unsure if she really wanted the nitty gritty details. But she could tell that he needed to get them out. He leaned back in his chair, but not far enough to pull his hand out from under hers.

"I got the call on my radio. I was only a few streets away, so I was the first one on the scene. When they called it in, I just had this feeling. And then they called in a black male, and his license plate number, so I knew it was him.  I just knew that he was going to be dead. I saw him, you know," he said.

"You did?" she asked. He nodded.

"He saw me, too. Just for a minute, before his eyes closed. But he saw me long enough for me to make it to him, and hold his hand. I tried to stop the bleeding, but it was pretty useless. The girl he saved, she was there, trying to help, but she had a concussion from when the bastard knocked her out.

Everything happened so fast, and before I knew it, the paramedics were there. But I like to think that maybe I gave him just a little bit of peace in that last moment," he said, his voice cracking a bit. He looked down at their hands on the table. She quickly retreated hers and wiped the tear that was streaming down her cheek.

"You did. I know you did," she said. "Man, I miss that guy."

"Me, too," he said. "I've barely slept a full night since it happened. I go in every day to see if there's any update on the bastard who did it. God, I'd give anything to find him. Anything."

She nodded. She hadn't given a ton of thought to the man who shot one of her best friends. It was too hard, knowing he was still out there, living his life after taking such a precious one away.

"So, now that I've put a total damper on the

evening," Dayton said, "shall we get to the elephant in the room?"

He stood from the table, holding his hand out toward the living room. She swallowed and followed him in.

"Yes, let's," she said. This was it. The culmination of the last three years. And she was dreading it, but not for the obvious reason that it would stir up the heartache. It was more because after tonight, after they had this conversation, Dayton and Luci, as she knew it, would be over. Not knowing the full story for three years had come with its challenges, but it had also allowed her to think now and again that this had all been some big misunderstanding. And despite all that he'd put her through, she knew that there was a small sliver of hope still alive somewhere inside of her. And after tonight, she'd have to extinguish it.

He led her to the couch, but walked past it toward the large wooden desk that sat in the corner of the room. He dug through the deep bottom drawer, his biceps flexing to lift a huge box from it and carry it to the coffee table in front of her. He sat down next to her, turning to face her fully.

"Luci, before we get to this," he said, motioning to the big brown box, "you have to promise me something."

She felt her heart rate accelerating. She could see the words "Property of Moore County Police" stamped in big red letters across the side of the box. On the top of the box was Dayton's last name, Briggs. Oh, God. What had he done?

"You have to promise me that you'll try not to think less of me after this. Well, less than you already do," he said, with his dangerous, half-smile.

"Okay," she said nervously. Jesus, just get *on* with it. He took a deep breath before pulling the top of the box off.

"I'm not technically supposed to have this," he said, "but I guess you can say I'm obsessed."

He pulled out the top file and flipped through it, pulling out a mugshot. The man in the picture looked strikingly like Dayton, just with a few more years of life behind his eyes, and in the wrinkles on his face. Same, steel-gray eyes, only, the eyes in the picture seemed to have a lot less life behind them than the eyes she'd stared into so many times.

"Is this your father?" she asked, taking the picture from him. He nodded. In all the years she'd been with him, she'd never once seen Mr. Briggs. She knew his name was Thomas, and that he'd left Dayton and his mother when Dayton was seven. And that was it. That was the extent of it. Dayton never spoke of him, and Luci never really felt like he suffered because of his missing father figure, so she left it alone. Why break something that didn't need fixing?

"So, what did he do?" she asked. Dayton swallowed and pulled out the next file.

"Do you remember Georgia Keats?" he asked. She nodded. Of course. She thought of Georgia anytime she went running at night, anytime she found herself walking to her car alone.

"DNA evidence has come a long way since we were kids," he said, pulling out another picture. It was a photo of a bright pink running tank top, laid out on a table, spattered in blood. It had to be Georgia's. Luci remembered the MISSING signs with Georgia's picture.

*Last seen heading onto the Dalesville Creek Trail. Wearing a pink tank top and black leggings*, they had read.

"That's not all hers," he said, pointing to the stains. He took a deep breath. "Some of it is my father's. We think she scratched him up pretty good when he attacked her."

Her eyes widened, realizing just what he was trying to tell her.

"My father killed Georgia Keats. The DNA evidence proves it," he said, the hand holding the photo starting to shake. She gasped, covering her mouth.

She had so many questions. She needed so many answers. But she didn't even know where to start.

"The conclusive evidence came back just as I was graduating from the academy. Right before. . . "

"Right before we were supposed to go to dinner," she said. He nodded.

"We've been looking for him ever since. Captain won't let me on the case, conflict of interest and whatnot, but he lets me keep tabs. They followed the money trail out to Arizona, and they think they've linked him to three other murders in three different states on the way. The FBI is getting involved now. They've been interviewing some of our distant relatives in Virginia. They have a lead on him down there, and they think they are close to nabbing him. When they catch him, they'll bring him back up here for trial."

Luci nodded, soaking it all in. She wasn't sure how she was supposed to react to that. "Congrats on catching your serial killer father," and "sorry your dad is going to jail forever," both seemed like equally shitty options.

"Does your mom know?" Luci asked after a few more moments of silence, studying the contents of the box, staring down at Georgia's senior picture. He nodded.

"They let me tell her, although, I don't know if that was better or not," he said.

"How did she take it?"

"I think, honestly, it brought her a little closure.

She finally knew why he ran out on us. Granted, it was to save his own ass because he's a fucking serial killer, but at least she knew. She had a reason. And when she told me that, I realized that I had done the same thing to you."

Luci's eyes found his for the briefest moment, but she dropped them fast. Yeah, she knew what it felt like to be abandoned. But she'd take a bad breakup any day over the love of her life being a cold-hearted killer. Comparing her own pain to his mother's felt a little cheap.

"You have to know something, Luci. You have to know that leaving you like that, the way I did, was the hardest thing I've ever done. But if I had to do it all again, I would. Because you deserve better than this. You deserve more than carrying this baggage around," he said, holding one of the files in the air and chucking it down on the table.

She didn't quite understand. He'd do it *again?* He'd put her through it *again?*

"But, you just took off," she said. He looked up at her.

"I know I did," he said. "Legally, I wasn't able to say anything because the case was still open. I'm still not really supposed to, but I just couldn't let you leave without explaining myself... again. But I also couldn't just carry on with us, knowing what I knew, knowing that someday this story was going to break, his name and face all over the news."

He stood up from the couch now, walking toward the back door. He ran one of his hands through his short hair, letting his fingers gently scratch the back of his neck. Finally, he turned back to her, and spoke again.

"How could I ask you to carry that? How could I ask you to take *his* last name?" He paused for a moment, staring blankly ahead. "That bastard took everything. Eventually, he even took you."

And suddenly, she saw something she had never seen, in all the years they were together, and that was Dayton Briggs crying. He had turned back toward the door, so she couldn't see his face. But she saw his shoulders shuddering, she saw his hand move to cover his face.

She stood up from the couch, walking toward him slowly at first, than as fast as her feet would carry her. She put one hand on his back first, then turned him to face her. She put her hands on his cheeks, using her thumbs to wipe away his tears. Her eyes searched his, waiting for him to come back to her.

"I'm so sorry, Luci," he said. "I'm so sorry."

Without hesitating, she wrapped her arms around his neck, standing on her tip-toes and pulling him into her, tight. She let her hand rub the back of his head, letting him get out what she knew he'd been holding in for three years. Finally, she pulled back ever so slightly, to look him in the eyes. Even red and tear-stained, his face was perfect.

And all the hate and hurt she had felt toward him, even just hours before, was melting away, turning into sadness and hurt *for* him. And to her surprise, that sliver of hope had grown into a full slice. She heard him swallow, and she realized just how close her face was to his. But instead of pulling away, she let her eyes scour his entire face, from his perfectly thick brows, to his steely eyes, to his pink and delicious lips. And she felt herself pulling him into her, taking his lips with her own.

He pulled back, purely out of surprise, to look at her for a moment.

"Oh, Luci," he whispered, running one of his strong hands through her dark ponytail. "I missed you so much. And I'm so, so sorry."

"Shh," she said, pushing against him again, this time, letting her tongue do the searching. She felt his grip around her waist tighten as a soft moan escaped from deep inside of him.

She had no idea what to say to him. She had no clue what words would help heal him. But she knew how to show him she still gave a shit. She knew how to show him that she'd thought of him every single day for the last three years. She knew how she'd show him that she still wanted him, despite who his father was, or what his father had done. She knew how she wanted to show him that she was giving up the stone-cold act she'd been putting on ever since she got back to Dalesville. Because even if he did leave her again, even if this was it, she was going to make it count. She'd survived it once. She could do it again.

It might not be the hate-sex Della had bet on, but it would be steamy nonetheless.

Shit. Della.

She jumped away from him and sprang across the room to her phone. He stared at her, one eyebrow raised, bulge in his pants.

"I'm sorry," she said, "I have to let Della know I'll be late."

She felt him coming closer, sliding his arms around her waist from behind.

"Let her know you'll be home tomorrow," he whispered in her ear, and she felt a trail of chills down her spine. She hit *send,* then let the phone slip out of her hand and onto the floor. His lips found hers again, pushing against hers hard.

# FIFTEEN
*Della*

As she paced around her empty house with her phone in her hand, she flicked it on, then off, then on again.

Della wanted to call her, but she had no idea what to say.

Then she heard his voice.

*Just do it, babe.*

She took a breath, then flipped the screen back on, dialing the number in the letter.

It rang a few times, and Della let out a sigh of relief. She didn't have to go through with it yet.

But then, Cora answered.

"Hello?" she asked. Della cleared her throat.

"H-hello, Cora?" she stammered. "This is Della Niles. Jackson's wife."

"Oh, oh my gosh, hi, Mrs. Niles," Cora said nervously. "It's so good to hear from you."

"Thanks. Listen, I'm sure you're busy right now, but I was wondering if you would be able to grab some coffee sometime soon," Della said, trying to sound more chipper than she was feeling.

"Oh, yes. That would be so nice. I'm actually just studying for an exam right now. I could be in Dalesville in forty-five minutes. Would that be okay?" she asked.

Gosh. Exams. Cora was still in college. Even though Della was only a few years older, it felt like they were a lifetime apart. Cora hadn't even begun to get into the sweet parts of her life yet. Or the sour parts.

"That's perfect. I'll meet you at the Music Café?"

"That sounds great. See you then!" she said.

Della took a breath before making her way to the bathroom to make herself look a little more presentable. She was about to have a conversation with one of the last people to see her husband alive.

The forty-five minutes passed incredibly fast, and before she knew it, Della found herself sitting at a table in the back of the Café.

She nervously drummed her fingertips across the table, darting her eyes toward the door every time it opened. Then finally, Cora appeared, her chocolate curls bouncing off her shoulders. She wore skinny jeans and a tight baby tee with a sweater pulled over it. She smiled shyly as she made eye contact with Della, making her way hurriedly to the table. Della rose to greet her, one hand on her belly.

"Cora," she said, trying to make her smile as warm as possible.

"Hi, Mrs. Niles," Cora said, reaching a hand out to accept Della's handshake. "Thank you so much for meeting with me."

"Call me Della, please," Della said, "and thank *you* for meeting with me. So, you have an exam coming up?" Cora nodded as she pulled out a chair and sat down.

"Yep, for one of my education classes. I'm in my junior year at Maryland."

"Ah, nice," Della said, taking a sip of her tea. "Education major?"

"Yes, I love it!" Cora said. Della smiled.

"I loved it too. I was a teacher before I got pregnant."

"Oh, wow, that's great! It's so rewarding," Cora said. Then an awkward silence fell over the table. Finally, Della spoke up again.

"Listen, Cora. I wanted to meet tonight because I read your letter," she said. Cora's eyes grew wide. "And I wanted to say something to you. I wanted to say I'm sorry. Through my own desperation and grief, I forgot that you were his victim, too. And I'm so sorry."

Cora swallowed loudly, then looked down at her hands on the table in front of her. After a moment, Della could see that she was fighting back tears. She reached across the table, taking Cora's hand in hers.

"I don't sleep anymore. I haven't since that night. And part of it is because the bastard's still on the loose. And part of it is because I feel so, *so* guilty. I think about your baby every single day," Cora said. Della instinctively put a hand to her bump. "I wake up wishing that I'd died in his place. Which sounds crazy, and a little dramatic. But this guilt I feel, it's so heavy. I can't shake it," Cora said, her voice just above a whisper. Della looked around. This was an oddly intimate conversation to have surrounded by a mass of people trying to enjoy their meals.

"Do you want to step outside?" Della asked. Cora nodded quickly, and they made their way to the patio.

Outside, they headed for the back of the patio, grabbing a table toward the back. They were the only two outside, seeing as it was the thick of Fall, but it was perfect.

"Listen to me," Della said, taking her hand again. "I know a thing or two about guilt." Cora looked up at her, one eyebrow raised. "Jackson went out that night because I wanted cheese fries."

Now Cora was staring at her, wide-eyed, like she couldn't tell whether or not Della was being serious. Della actually cracked a smile.

"I know, it's ridiculous. But my first trimester, and into my second, I was so sick, I could barely keep anything down. So whenever I'd actually *want* to eat something, we'd jump on the chance. And I woke up that night *starving.* So he went out to get them for me."

Cora nodded slowly.

"So I've spent God knows how many nights laying in our bed, wishing I'd just let him sleep, sucked it up, waited till morning," Della said. Cora nodded again, looking down at the ground.

"But then I read your letter," Della said, and Cora's eyes met hers. "And I realized that if I had, if I'd let him sleep, he wouldn't have been there for you. He wouldn't have been able to save you. I don't know what you believe in—Jackson and I weren't the most religious—but I believe things happen for a reason. And I realized that Jackson, he wouldn't want me to hold that guilt. Not for me, not for our son."

Cora's eyes widened again, and Della smiled.

"Oh, yeah. It's a boy," she said, rubbing her belly.

"Congratulations!" Cora said, her voice cracking and she sniffled.

"Listen to me, Cora," Della said, growing serious again, "you've got to let go of that guilt. You've got to realize that you were saved for a reason. Maybe you don't know what it is yet, but the beauty is, now you get to figure it out. And my Jackson, he would *not* want you to sink yourself with that. He would want you to keep living."

As Della said the words, she felt a bolt of clarity run through her.

Because Jackson would want the exact same thing for Della, too. He'd want her to keep living for herself. For him. And for their son.

Cora smiled through the tears streaming down her face. Della blinked, and realized they were streaming down hers, too.

"Thank you," Cora said, throwing her arms around Della's neck. Della squeezed her right back. "Della?"

"Hmm?"

"Can we meet again, sometime? I'd like to hear more about Jackson. About what he was like," Cora said. A smile spread across Della's face.

"I would absolutely love that," she said, looking up to the sky. "And so would he."

# SIXTEEN
## Luci

Luci's fingers danced through Dayton's hair, and to her pleasant surprise, there was still enough left for her to hold on to as his tongue made its path down her neck.

He pushed her up against the wall behind her, lifting her arms above her head, and letting his fingers trail down them. He tilted her chin up with one finger, looking into her eyes again before kissing her.

She wrapped her arms around his neck, her legs following suit around his waist. His hands slid up her thighs slowly, making their way past the hem of her dress, and she clenched tighter around him. He spun her in slow circles as they kissed, and she was overcome with impatience.

Enough with the kissing, already. Three years. *Three* years, dammit!

She pulled away from his mouth, letting hers fall back on his neck, nibbling it gently, a weakness of his that she remembered.

"Luci," he whispered, and she smiled, her tongue and teeth unrelenting.

She slid down his body, letting her hands slide toward the bottom of his shirt, pulling it out from his jeans. Her fingers found each button with little-to-no effort, and she beamed with pride at how fast she was undressing him. When his shirt was off, she reached down and pulled off his undershirt, exposing a stronger, broader version of the chest she remembered. She left a trail of kisses across it as he tilted his head up toward the ceiling. Finally, he stopped her, twirling her around in front of him. He reached around her, his fingers finding the bow of her halter top around her neck and loosening it in one pull as his lips worked their magic on hers.

Her dress fell to the floor in one quick motion, puddling at her feet. She stood in front of him, for the first time in three years, in nothing but her bra and underwear. He licked his lips at the sight of her, and she couldn't help but smile.

He scooped her up again, and she let her legs wrap back around his waist, pulling his groin into hers. He carried her back through the kitchen, lying her down on the table. Her hands found his belt buckle, undoing it with such impatience that she was afraid she'd break it. She reached for his button, then his zipper, letting his jeans fall to the floor.

Even through his boxers, she could see just how *much* he'd missed her. She pulled him down toward her, letting their tongues meet again. He reached around, unclasping her bra, and throwing it across the room. His mouth found all parts of her, and she remembered this feeling so clearly. The feeling of being totally lost, totally unaware of her surroundings. All she was aware of was him.  His fingers slid down to her panty line, and she thought she might have audibly whimpered. Then he twiddled them across her navel before slipping down into her panties, then inside her, finding the right spot in no time.

Their muscle memory was impeccable; the way their bodies moved in such sync, the way hers reacted to his. Finally, he slid his fingers out and let them pull her underwear down her legs slowly.

They probably could have gone to the bedroom, but that wouldn't have exactly been the hot, spontaneous, long-awaited makeup sex she knew they had *both* been pining for. The prospect of making love to Dayton again had been so out of the realm of possibility just days ago, that it was a literal fantasy. She wasn't about to get practical about it.

He reached around her thighs, pulling her to the edge of the table. To her pleasure, she was at the perfect height. He pushed her back so that she was flush against the table, and she closed her eyes, bracing for the glorious impact.

He moved inside of her with one perfect thrust, and she felt her whole body react, each of her senses heightening.

When he'd left her, at the ripe old age of twenty-two, she'd still partially seen him as a boy. The same boy she had loved since she was eighteen. The same boy who she'd done it all with.

But it was clear to her at this moment, that Dayton Briggs had very much become a *man.*

He reached down and wrapped a hand around her head, pulling her face up toward his. She wrapped her arms around him, biting his chest gently as he moved like a freaking expert.

He scooped her up, still inside her, carrying her into the living room without missing a beat, and she wrapped her arms and legs around him tight, each step sending vibrations through her body. He stopped at the couch, letting his hands find her breasts before setting her down to stand on the ground. He pulled her toward the arm of the couch, bending her over slightly before taking her from behind. She shrieked with pleasure; having the freedom to move about the house was something she had never gotten to experience with Dayton. They'd both still lived with their parents when he left, and they were forced to sneak around behind any closed door they could find. Lurking mothers didn't exactly work wonders for their sex life. This was *so* much better than doing it in the back of his truck, or rushing through it before her mom got home from work.

He turned her back around, easing her down onto the couch. As he lowered himself on top of her, he paused, his forehead against hers.

"Are you okay?" she asked, trying to be patient, but also trying not to lose sight of the oh-so-amazing promise land she was headed for. He nodded.

"I have never stopped loving you," he said.

Before she could say anything back, he was inside of her again, drawing her closer and closer to the brink. She wrapped her legs around him tight, afraid that if she let go, he'd somehow disappear. She dug her fingernails into his shoulders and he moved. He moved once, twice, three times before stopping. Damn it, she was almost there. So close. That's okay, maybe next time. This had happened with Charlie a lot, too.

But Dayton wasn't done. He just remembered what she needed. He remembered what her body wanted. He reached his hand down, letting it move in perfect circles on her most precious parts, like the expert that he was. She felt the electricity resparking inside of her, and to her surprise, she felt it picking up right where it had left off. His hand was moving faster now, one circle to the next, as his other hand crept around her body, giving her butt a squeeze.

His lips trailed down her lips, to her neck, to her chest, taking her in his mouth as fingers moved, as if they were conducting a Goddamn orchestra inside of her.

Holy. Freaking. Shit.

"Dayton. *Dayton!*" she heard herself saying, biting down hard on her lip. Then, he entered her again. He went deeper, faster, than he had before, his hand still moving on her, taking her from every angle. He moved once, twice, before letting out a long, *insanely* sexy moan.  As he drew himself into her with one last motion, she felt herself imploding. Her body shuddered around his, his hand finally quitting after her surrender.

He laid one more kiss on her lips before pulling himself up next to her. He wrapped his whole body around hers, pulling the big, brown throw from the top of the couch onto them.

She curled up against him and breathed him in. It had been so long since she'd laid her head on his chest. She let her fingers trace the lines on his tattoos— his mother's initials, and a sun that he'd gotten after graduation. And as her hand danced across his skin, it landed on a new one, one she'd never seen. The initials "JJN" were scrolled in thick, black letters.

Jackson.

She circled them with her fingers, then pulled his face to hers for a long kiss.

"I get why you did it," she said after a few minutes of silence. "I get why you left. But I need to know something."

"What's that?"

"How could you think that that would be enough for me to not want you? How could you think that I was better off?"  she asked, pushing herself up. He sat up, too, scooting slightly away from her. "I didn't want *his* last name. I wanted *yours,*" she said, and she saw his eyes widen. "I appreciate the sentiment, I appreciate you trying to shield me, protect my honor or whatever. But you don't get to decide what I deserve."

"But, Luci," he said, swiveling around so that his feet were on the floor, "this is going to get so, so ugly. My name will be everywhere. People will associate me with him for the rest of my life. How can I let you go through that, too?" She scooted closer to him, lacing her fingers in his.

"You just might not have a choice," she said with a smile. After a moment, his face broke into his quicksand smile, and if she hadn't still been recovering from the first round, she probably would have jumped him again.

"I'm stuck with you then, huh? Is that what you're saying?" he said, pulling her into him. She nodded.

"Yep. You can't get rid of me again," she laughed, kissing his cheek and throwing her legs across him. Suddenly, his face grew serious as he pulled her in tight.

"I was never rid of you, Luci. I've thought about you every day since I left that stupid letter in your mailbox. All I've ever wanted was just to know that you're happy."

She pushed herself onto him, straddling him, and kissed him, hard.

"Mission accomplished," she said.

Luci opened her eyes slowly, squinting in the sunlight that was streaming through Dayton's back door. They were still on the couch, rolled up in the blanket, his arms wrapped around her. She took a moment to memorize his face, stare at all the curves and edges of him, gently run her fingers through his hair. But she was jolted back to reality at the obnoxious sound of her phone alarm, jingling and buzzing away on the floor where she had tossed it the night before.

She scurried off the couch, still stark naked, to grab it before it woke him up. *Shit.* She had forgotten all about Della's sonogram appointment today. At this rate, she'd have no time to go wash up. She was familiar with the walk of shame—she'd experienced it a handful of times back in Seattle as she hurriedly rushed back to her apartment from Charlie's in the same clothes she had been wearing the night before.

This had to be the first time in history, though, that someone did the walk of shame into a thirty-week sonogram appointment.

She shot off a quick *I'll be a few minutes late* text to Della, then began scouring the room for her belongings.

She crept around his living room and into the kitchen, locating her bra, which was hanging off of one of the chairs, her underwear, bunched up next to the table, and her dress, still in a heap on the kitchen floor. Jesus, it looked like they were animals last night, starving for sex, with no time for organization of any sort. She slipped her shoes on, bending over to buckle them, and she heard him whistle.

She smiled, slowly straightening up as she sauntered toward him.

"Off so soon?" he asked, reaching an arm around her as she sat on the couch next to him.

"I totally forgot that Della has an appointment today," she said. "But, uh, I'm kinda stranded here."

He smiled, hopping up from the couch to grab his jeans off the desk chair. She practically melted at the site of his tight cheeks before they disappeared behind the denim.

The car ride to the doctor's office was quiet, but perfect. Like they were both still basking in their new-found moves from the night before. When they finally pulled up to the door, he leaned in for a long kiss over the center console.

"Can I see you later?" she asked.

He smiled, locking a hand in her hair and pulling her lips to his again.

"Luce, you can see me whenever you want to. I'm not going anywhere," he whispered.

She smiled, kissing his forehead before hopping up.

"Good," she said. "Now, get some rest. You might need it if there's going to be a Part Two of last night."

She winked just before she shut the door.

# SEVENTEEN
## *Della*

Della sat on the edge of the table, paper gown tied loosely around her enormous bump.

She stared at herself in the mirror that hung from the back of the door, and she wondered why they even put mirrors in here in the first place.

As if pregnancy didn't already provide enough surprises when it came to her own body, they had to go and force her to wear what was essentially a large piece of tissue paper while she waited for someone to scope out her vagina. The damn gown tore slightly if she even *breathed* too hard, and she noticed how ironic it was, as she shifted it around awkwardly, that they didn't make maternity-size tissue paper gowns, even though the majority of people wearing them would be pregnant women.

She stood up straight, gauging just how far her belly was sticking out now. Another fun surprise came in the last week in the form of her belly button popping out of its rightful place, making sure that any and all of her somewhat form-fitting clothes remained on their hangers for the rest of her pregnancy.

The horrific stretch marks had started making their way down her legs a bit now, as if their conquest of her midriff wasn't sufficient enough. There were even some sprouting around her boobs, now, and her nipples had grown and stretched into long, flat, saucers. Her body as she knew it was quickly disappearing, as if to remind her that no part of her was her own anymore, and hadn't been in quite some time.

But as she examined her new self, she smiled. Because a tiny foot to her ribcage reminded her what was coming.

To her surprise, the door to her room burst open as a panting Luci stepped inside.

"I'm so sorry I missed the sonogram!" she cried.

Della leaned back on one heel, arms crossed above the bump, tapping her foot with her eyebrows raised.

"So, how was the hate-sex?" Della asked. Luci finally caught her breath as a smile crept over her face.

"There was no hate-sex," she said, sinking down onto the chair in the corner of the room. Della's eyes were pleading. How could there not be hate-sex?

"There was really hot make-up sex, though." Luci said, staring down at her fingernails casually before lifting her eyes to Della.

Della spun in circles, throwing her fists around in an uncoordinated pregnant dance move, and Luci burst into a fit of laughter.

"Oh my *God!*" Della cried. "I need details, woman. I haven't had sex in months, and let's be honest, *this,*" she said, pointing down to her crotch, "will likely be closed for business for a long time in a few weeks."

Just as Luci was about to open her mouth, there

was a knock on the door. Della hurried back to the table, as if the doctor couldn't know she had done anything but sit and wait patiently for her to appear.

"Good morning, ladies," Dr. Malloy said, coming in and closing the door. "How are we feeling, mama?"

Della smiled. At first, the whole "mama" thing weirded her out. She didn't have a kid yet—at least, not one that lived outside of her—and it felt a little premature. But suddenly, she was starting to feel a sense of pride, a sense of readiness. She had no idea where it was coming from, but she liked it.

"I'm feeling pretty good," she said, rubbing her belly through her tissue-paper gown. "I'll be even better if you tell me the cyst is gone," she said.  Dr. Malloy smiled, opening Della's file and pulling out the new sonogram pictures from earlier that morning.

She examined them closely, and Della felt her heart rate picking up. Luci reached for her hand, able to tell immediately that her nerves were winning their battle.

What if it wasn't shrinking?

Then it would shrink by the next appointment, she told herself.

But she only had a few weeks left. This thing needed to disappear. And *now*.

"Well, I have some good news," Dr. Malloy said, rolling closer to Della on the table. "Here's a photo from your last sonogram," she said, circling the cyst with her red pen, "and here's this week's. You can see, the cyst has shrunk by half its size."

Della felt a wave of relief, but she knew she wasn't safely on the shore just yet.

"So, you think it will be gone?"

"I'd be surprised if it wasn't gone by the next appointment, but there's a chance it might stick around a little longer. We will check on it again in two weeks," she said, closing the file.

Della hated Dr. Malloy's vagueness, particularly when it came to the brain of her unborn child.

*It could be gone, it might not be. It should be, but who knows.*

She may as well have said she had no freaking idea. But Della nodded and thanked her as she left the room. Like the mind-ninja that she was, Luci stepped into her line of view.

"It's going to be fine, Della Bee. Don't be angry with her. She's only human, after all."

Della sighed. Luci was *always* right. It was annoying.

"Okay, fine. Distract me. Tell me about your night," Della said. And she recognized a sudden shift in Luci as they walked out of the office. Some sort of guard went up, but she just wasn't sure what it was for, or, *who* she was guarding.

"It went really well," Luci said.

"Well, *obviously,* since it involved hot make-up sex. But what did you guys talk about? What were his reasons? Are you getting back together?" Della asked, realizing she sounded like a group of reporters at a press conference.

Luci looked down to her hands, fumbling with her keys, and Della suddenly realized that Luci hadn't quite answered some of these questions for herself yet either.

"I don't think I can. . .I don't think I can say," Luci finally said, standing awkwardly next to her car. Della looked up at her. Withholding information from each other wasn't something they had a whole lot of experience with.

When Della and Jackson found out they were pregnant, they'd agreed to keep it to themselves until she reached the end of her first trimester. Partially because of the risks associated with the first few weeks, and partially because it was fun having this massive secret that only the two of them shared.

But all the while, Della had been *dying* to call Luci. They had never kept anything from each other, especially nothing life-changing. The day she and Jackson had first had sex in his mom's basement, Della had called Luci. When Luci decided to move to Seattle, Della was right there with her, holding her hand and telling her to spread her wings. When Della's mom was diagnosed, Luci held her like she was a small child while she cried until she fell asleep.

"Okay. . ." Della said, trying to drum up the next words. "Can you just tell me, is it bad? Is he okay?"

Luci nodded, still fumbling with her keys.

"I just can't tell you yet. It's related to a. . .a case that he's working on. I have a feeling you'll know soon," Luci said. "Everyone will."

Della contemplated quietly for a moment, wondering whether or not she should press for more, or let it sit until Luci was ready. She sighed, reaching for Luci's hand.

"Can you just tell me if you want him back or not?" she asked. A smile spread across Luci's face, and Della saw a tear twinkling in her eye.

"I do," she said, just above a whisper. "I know you've known this, but I never *didn't* want him back."

Della smiled, pulling her in for a hug, although, all embraces these days were awkward, one-armed ones. No one could fit over the belly anymore.

"I'm so happy for you, Luce. So did you guys talk about things? Are you officially back together?"

"We didn't have 'the talk,' because, well, we're not sixteen," she said with a sarcastic smile, and Della shot her a look. "But let's just say, I don't think either of us is going anywhere, unless the other is in tow."

Della pushed off of her car and wrapped Luci in a hug again.

In the two decades plus that they had been friends, Della had never seen Luci struggle the way she had after Dayton. And although on the outside Della told her she didn't need him, that there were other fish in the sea, she didn't fully believe it herself.

Mostly, because Dayton was pretty perfect. He let Luci do her own thing, adoring her all the while. He was perfect for Luci, just like Jackson was perfect for Della.

Jackson.

As she hugged Luci hard, fully embracing the fact that her friend was back to being in love and happy, she was also letting go of the comfort of camaraderie she had felt for the last few months.

For the first time since she was seventeen, Della was alone and, technically, single. She had joined a new club—well, "joined" was a pretty liberal term; really she was thrust into it with no other option—but it was a club where Luci was a member, and was waiting for her.

They had made their lesbian couple jokes, laughed at the idea of growing old together with no ounce of testosterone in sight.

But now, with Dayton back, Della had to face the idea of being alone, well, *alone.*

"Come on," Luci said, "don't make me cry in this parking lot. Let's get home."

The next morning, though she managed to sleep in a bit, Della succumbed to her ever-shrinking bladder for the fifth time since she had laid down. She decided to save herself the effort of getting back in bed. She trudged through her bathroom, scooting the scale out from behind the vanity and stepping up onto it. Yes, she had just been weighed less than 24 hours ago at the doctor, but again, she refused to look or ask. She knew she wouldn't be able to hide the horror in her eyes if she heard the number, and she couldn't handle the office staff judging her for being so vain.

"You're *pregnant,*" Jackson had told her, so many moons ago. "You're *supposed* to gain weight. Stop worrying about it; don't even look at the scale."

Just as she nudged the stupid scale back into its place, there was a knock at her bathroom door. Luci stepped in, holding a beautifully wrapped gift box.

"What is this?" Della asked.

"Open it," Luci said.

Della did what she was told, carefully removing the perfectly tied bow that she knew Luci had done herself. She pulled out a wine-colored dress, cinched at the waist like her other maternity clothes. But this didn't *feel* like a maternity dress. It had spaghetti straps and a delicate beaded sash around the bust line. It felt like a *real* dress.

"What is this for?" she asked.

"Put it on, and come downstairs in one hour," Luci told her. "Relax up here; there's breakfast on the bed. Watch some T.V., read a book. But *don't* look out the window," she said, then disappeared.

Della did as she was told, happily partaking in the relaxation. Sleep had grown broken and unrestful in the last few weeks, as the weight of the baby pushed down hard on everything else inside of her. No position was comfortable for longer than an hour, and, like clockwork, when she found one that brought her some comfort, it was time to pee again.

Finally, she stepped in front of the mirror, pulling the dress on and tying the sash behind her. For being the size of a small elephant, she actually looked pretty good.

She'd heard the front door open and shut a few times, but she obeyed Luci and didn't peek. She tried to figure out who was coming, but all she heard were the distant sounds of whispers.

She wondered if it was Cash. He hadn't been home in a few weeks. But why the dress? Maybe just because Luci knew how frumpy she had been feeling. After an hour had passed, she took a breath and one last look in the mirror before heading out into the hallway. She slowly made her way down the steps, bracing herself for whatever the surprise was. At the bottom of the steps stood Luci, all dolled up, looking as beautiful as ever.

"Let's go," she said, holding her hand out. They turned the corner into the living room, and that's when Della saw everything.

Huge, pale green and blue balloons at every corner, tied to all the chairs.

An elegant spread of finger foods, fruit and veggie platters, delicious desserts, and punch.

A pile of presents that just about reached the ceiling.

All of her friends, her mother-in-law and sister-in-law, her Aunt Bea, her cousins. Mrs. Ruiz, Bria, Olivia, Jamie. All sitting around her living room on her couches and chair, smiling, waiting for her to arrive to her surprise baby shower.

She burst into tears.

They surrounded her, giving her hugs and kisses, asking how she was feeling, touching her bump. At least five of them told her about the "glow," she had, although, she insisted each time that it was just sweat.

"Alright, everyone," Luci said, using her best executive voice, "let's do gifts!"

Luci led Della to the chair in the corner of the room, decorated with the most balloons, including one that said "MOM," on it.

Bria sat in front of her with a notepad, ready to be the scribe.

For what seemed like the next year, Della sat while Luci handed her gift after gift. She opened the most adorable clothes she'd ever seen, and immediately shot down her prior notion that boy clothes weren't as cute as girl clothes.

She opened a bassinet from Mrs. Ruiz, a diaper pail from Olivia, and a changing pad from Mrs. Pete, their nosey, but sinfully sweet neighbor.

And then, Luci handed her a big, flat box from the bottom of the pile.

"That's from me," Elyse said, quietly. Della looked at her mother-in-law for a moment, overjoyed that she had made the trip to Dalesville. Her dark skin was even darker than the last time she'd seen her, Della knew because she gardened like a fiend every summer and early fall.

Elyse's hair was pulled back into a bun, and Della noticed that her normally kind eyes seemed a little harder today. Probably for the same reason that Della's had hardened—they'd seen unfathomable loss.

Elyse leaned forward in her chair, hands folded neatly in her lap. Whenever Elyse was surrounded by Della's friends and family, Della got the feeling that she felt a little out of place. Maybe it was because she didn't know what her role was, now that Della's mother was gone. She didn't want to overstep her boundaries, which Della understood.

But Della couldn't help but be bothered by Elyse's tendency to shut herself off from the gatherings, sit quietly by herself. She didn't want her to feel left out. She didn't want her to be alone. She wanted her to feel like family. Because she was. And now, she was one of the only people Della had left.

Della lifted the top off the box, handing it to Luci. She tore off the tissue paper, unveiling a beautiful handmade quilt. It was made up of hundreds of little squares in various shades of blue and yellow, all cut and sewn into one perfect blanket.

She traced her fingers around the stitching, and she stopped, as her fingers landed on a message stitched right into the quilt.

*My Daddy, My Guardian Angel,* it read, in impeccably-stitched blue thread.

She felt her hand trembling above it, as she lifted her eyes to Elyse's. Tears streamed down Della's face as she pushed herself up, not-so-gracefully, and walked across the room. Elyse stood up to meet her halfway, and Della took her into her arms, burying her face in her mother-in-law's shoulder.

"It's beautiful," she whispered. "I love it. Thank you so much."

"Of course, baby," Elyse said, rubbing her back. Behind them, Luci continued on with the party, encouraging everyone to grab some food before the games started. But Della stood for a few moments more, her arms wrapped around the woman who raised the perfect man.

"How do I do this?" she asked, sitting down on the couch. Elyse sat next to her, still holding her hand.

"Oh, baby, let me tell you something. No one knows what they're doing when it comes to parenting. They might think they have it all figured out, but in truth, *no one* does," she said.

"But you did. I mean, look how perfect Jackson turned out. And Jeanie, too," Della said, rubbing her belly and admiring her gorgeous sister-in-law, who was effortlessly making small talk with women she didn't know.

Jeanie was three years older than Jackson, and

although they'd gone to high school for a short period together, she and Della had never really been close, simply because they never had a chance to be. Jeanie went off to college in South Carolina before Della and Jackson even started dating, and had never come back. She'd fallen in love with her southern roots, and moved closer to their family there. She was married with no kids, and no plans to have any. But she was the principal of a high school just outside York, and had won awards for her work in the surrounding underserved communities. Jeanie reminded Della of Luci in the way that she persevered through everything and anything; the words "I can't," were simply just not in her vocabulary.

And then there was Elyse's perfect, sweet, sensitive, strong Jackson.

"Baby, nobody is perfect. Not even my babies," she said with a smile. "You will be learning for the rest of your life. Shoot, I'm still learning how to be a mother some days. ...But if you ever need anything. You call me. I'll do my best to help you, baby."

"Thank you, Elyse," Della said, squeezing her hand.

When the party was over, Della tried to put food in baggies and collect bowls, but she was shooed off to the couch each time.

"Get off your feet, woman," Luci said, scurrying past her to grab the vacuum. Finally, when everything was spick and span, neater than it was before the party, Luci sunk into the couch next to Della.

"*That,*" Della said, "was amazing. I can't believe you and your mom did all of this. Seriously. I can't thank you enough."

"Oh, stop it," Luci said, waving her hand. "It was so much fun. We would have done more, but it sort of snuck up on me that you're in your last trimester. This kid is going to be here soon!"

Della smiled and nodded, rubbing her bump.

It really was coming fast. And before she knew it, she'd be on this couch, holding a tiny version of Jackson, not knowing what she was doing.

Jackson.

Sweet Jackson would miss it all.

# EIGHTEEN
*Luci*

Luci was standing over the stove, flipping pancakes for whenever Della made her way downstairs. The shower had been a huge hit, and Luci was proud of how everything turned out. There was still enough leftover cake in the fridge to feed a small army, but she knew Cash would have no trouble finishing that off when he got home today.

His semester was finally out, leaving him with just barely a month break. And he planned to spend it all with Della.

Luci loved Cash, almost like he was her own brother. He was such a good kid, even growing up. He stayed out of Della's things, never bothered her and Luci when they wanted privacy, and never embarrassed them in front of friends or boys. In fact, Luci couldn't remember a single argument between Della and Cash for their entire childhood. She'd spent so much time with the two of them. . .especially after her father was deported.

It was almost two decades ago, but Luci could still remember it, clear as day.

Her father, Raul, had parked illegally while running into the post office on his lunch break. An officer stopped and was waiting at his car when he returned. Raul was on his way to becoming a citizen by marriage, but his green card hadn't been fully processed yet. And because he'd entered the country illegally before marrying her mother, the traffic violation made him "inadmissible," meaning, he wouldn't be granted his green card. Within days, ICE arrived at their house, taking her father out in handcuffs, and shipping him off to Cuba. And all for double-parking for a minute and twenty-three seconds.

After that, Luci, Cash and Della were inseparable. When Cash and Della's mother passed, and then their father, the three of them clung to each other even stronger. After all, what they knew of family was dwindling away.

As Luci reminisced and flipped the cakes on the griddle, she heard the front door open.

"Mornin'!" Cash called, setting his bags down in the foyer. He hopped into the kitchen, dropping a kiss on Luci's cheek as he snatched a pancake off the plate, letting it dance in his fingers to cool off a bit.

"Mmm," he said, taking a massive bite. She laughed and shook her head.

"Welcome home!" she said. "How was the drive?"

"It was fine," he said, pulling out a chair at the table. "There's never any traffic on Saturdays. So, I heard you and Dayton were back together."

He said it casually as he munched on his food, scarfing it down as if he hadn't eaten in days. She rolled her eyes.

"You Mears kids can't keep anything quiet, can

you?" she asked. He chuckled and shook his head.

"I'm glad things are better. I like Dayton," he said. She smiled.

"Me, too. So, what are you guys doing today?" she asked him. They'd conceived the plan about a week before, late on the phone one night after Della had crashed on the couch, a bag of Hershey's kisses resting on her belly.

"I was thinking I'd take her to have some lunch, and then I made her an appointment for a prenatal massage. Then, we're going to go to Aunt Bea's for dinner, which we both know could take hours." She laughed.

"Sounds perfect," she said. "You are an excellent partner."

About an hour later, Della appeared, dressed in her most comfortable pair of yoga pants, and one of Dayton's big t-shirts. Her golden hair was up in a messy bun, curly wisps dropping out everywhere. But she looked good, rested. Luci reheated her pancakes as the three of them sat, waiting for her to be done, laughing at memories of their childhood.

Finally it was time for them to go. Luci said goodbye, waited for the car to be out of sight, then grabbed her phone.

"Hello?" his familiar, scruffy voice said. She smiled at just the sound of it, and she could almost hear him saying her name, the way he had moaned it just a few nights earlier. She shivered.

"Hey," she said. "They are gone. Do you want to bring it over?"

"Yep, already have it in my truck. I'll be there in about five minutes."

She couldn't wait. Partially because she was so excited to surprise Della again. Luci had ordered the perfect crib and dresser earlier that week, and Dayton had offered to pick it up, and help her put it together.

Cash was going to take her out, and keep her out, all day while they set everything up in the nursery, just as Jackson had planned it.

Luci also couldn't wait to see Dayton again. It had been a few days, and she was craving him in every way imaginable.

Finally, she heard his tires roll up and his engine cut off. She watched from the porch as he lifted the back hatch, sliding one huge box out from the truck. He carried it up the steps, and she pointed him in the direction of the nursery, noticing all the while his muscles, braced and bulging from his sleeves, and his tattoos peeking out. She fanned herself. He went back to the car for a second trip, this time carrying in two boxes at once. He set them down on the ground and looked around. Then, he looped an arm around her waist, pulling her into him, and kissing her, long and hard.

"I missed you," he said, finally peeling himself off of her. She smiled, collecting herself and straightening out her shirt.

"Okay, so," she said, unfolding the piece of paper, Jackson's scribbles all over it. "I got the paint all set up. I thought we could paint the walls, and then build the furniture in the other room, and carry it in when everything dries." He nodded.

"Good plan," he said.

She liked painting, but she didn't get to do it often. She rented her apartment in Seattle, so she couldn't do it there. When she still lived at home, her parents gave her free reign to do what she wanted with her room. She had painted it so many times since high school, choosing a color, painting, and growing sick of it in a year.

Jackson had picked out a soft blue for three of

the walls, and a soft yellow for the wall behind the crib. She smiled as she painted, thinking of the quilt Jackson's mother had made. It matched the colors perfectly, and she knew Elyse had been working on that quilt for months, keeping in line with her son's vision.

"This looks really good," Dayton said after a little while, standing back and admiring their work. They had two-and-a-half walls done, and agreed to stop for a break.

They went down to the kitchen, where Luci whipped up two of her famous grilled cheese sandwiches, complete with a glass of Della's lemonade.

"Thank you for helping me with all of this," she said, leaning back against the patio chair, letting the summer wind blow through her messy, paint-speckled hair.

"Of course," he said. "Although, it's really all Jackson's idea, I guess." She smiled and nodded.

Aside from the kiss when he first arrived, they had actually been keeping their distance most of the morning. She could have been reading too much into it; it was more than likely just because they both knew they only had a day to get the nursery done. But she couldn't help but feel like there was some sort of invisible wall between them, one that Dayton, in particular, was afraid to scale.

But she knew why. She knew he was holding onto guilt for leaving her behind. And guilt for what lied ahead of them, and what she was volunteering to take on with him.

She so badly wanted to pounce on him, right here, on the patio, with Della's nosey neighbor probably lurking behind a bush. But she felt herself holding back, too. They were still the same two people, but this relationship, this was all new. They were older. They had lives, homes, stories that the other hadn't even played a part in. They were going to have to figure it out. But as long as he was a part of the sequel, she was ready for it.

After lunch, they headed back upstairs to the nursery to finish their paint job. Next, Dayton followed Luci into her room, where the baby's furniture lie in boxes, scattered around the floor. In no time, Dayton had the boxes emptied and the pieces lined up, ready to be assembled.

"I don't remember you being so handy back in the day," Luci said, admiring the swiftness with which he screwed two pieces of the crib together. He smirked.

"I don't think following directions and putting together pieces out of a box can be considered 'handy,'" he said, "but I've learned a thing or two from working on the house."

"Yeah. I can tell. You're definitely good with your hands. . . in more ways than one," she said. She watched as his dangerous smile stretched across his lips, his eyes never leaving the screwdriver in front of him.

She was going to scale that wall, if it took all the dirty euphemisms in the book.

Within an hour, the crib was built and set up. It was on wheels, so it would be fairly easy to move into the nursery once the paint had dried.

As they moved on to assembling the dresser, he requested piece by piece, tool by tool, and she handed him just what he needed, licking her lips with desire as he hammered and screwed away. He moved back, glancing down at the directions for a second, then stood up.

"Okay," he said. "Almost done. You hold these pieces together. . ." he said, moving her toward the wood. She held them tight, but as he moved around her, adding the final touches with his impressive force, she felt her grip weakening. She needed him to be hammering and screwing *her.* Finally, he relieved her of her position, his handy work keeping everything in place.

"Done?" she asked. He nodded, brushing his hands off and pushing himself up.

"Almost," he said, taking a step toward her. Now *he* was the one licking his lips. Ha. Seemed like those dirty euphemisms worked, after all.

He reached down to the bottom of her old, worn, paint-covered tank top and yanked it off over her head. She returned the favor, removing his shirt. She could feel the nerves in her body begin to work in overtime, as if each of them was gearing up for its own tiny orgasm.

His tongue moved on hers, his lips overpowering. He picked her up, carrying her toward her bed. He swatted at the boxes and plastic, making room for her, and gently laid her down. But as she remembered their last encounter, she decided it was her turn to run things. She quickly jumped up, using all her strength to turn him around, forcing him down on the bed. She straddled him, grabbing a fistful of his hair and pulling his head back. She let her tongue draw circles, spell words, practically dance the salsa across his neck, his moans making it vibrate.

She stopped and leaned back for a moment, pulling her sports bra up over her head and letting it fall to the floor. She loved the way he looked at her, like he was in total awe, so grateful, so thankful for what was in front of him. And *so* damn hungry for it.

She dragged her fingers down his chest, letting them dip into the divots of his abs, until they reached his button. She teased him for a moment, pulling on it without undoing it. She slipped one finger down into his pants, then another, then another, further and further, until she felt all of him.

As hard as the wood of the dresser they'd been hammering all morning.

But to her surprise, she found his hand mimicking her own, slipping further and further down into her pink thong until it reached its destination.

And then her phone rang, ringing and vibrating wildly in her pocket, and she jumped. If it were *anyone* else, she would have ignored it. She would have snapped the damn phone in two. If it wasn't playing "You're My Best Friend" by Queen, her ringtone for Della since they were in eighth grade, she would have given up technology entirely in that moment, if it meant Dayton's hands could stay in her pants. She sighed, cursing Father Time himself, and hopped off of Dayton, hitting the answer button.

"Della Bee? What's up?" she asked.

But the voice that answered was deeper than she expected. "It's Cash," he said, and she didn't have to see his face to recognize the worry.

"What's going on?"

"We were on the way to the spa when she felt these really sharp pains. When we got there, she was bleeding a little bit. We're on the way to the hospital now," he told her.

"Okay. I'll be there in fifteen minutes," she said. Before she even hung up the phone, Dayton was dressing himself, and handing her her shirt.

"I can drive," he said, "I have my car."

They rushed out of the house, not even taking a moment to mourn the sexcapade that never was.

Luci was quiet the whole way to the hospital, as Dayton weaved through traffic on the highway. She'd never ridden in a cop car before, and if she weren't worried sick, she probably would have taken the time to explore it, asking him what everything on the dashboard did, wanting to try the siren.

"Hey," he said, reaching over and lacing his fingers with hers, "it's going to be okay."

At the hospital, Dayton grabbed a chair in the waiting room with Cash as Luci made her way back to Della's room. Della lie on the bed, her hospital gown open to expose her belly. She had some sort of monitor attached to her, reading the baby's heart rate. Despite the fear in her eyes, she smiled when she saw Luci.

"Hi," she said.

"Hey," Luci answered, kissing her forehead and sitting down in the chair next to her. "What are they saying?"

"They did a sonogram and are monitoring his heartbeat for a little bit. Dr. Malloy is supposed to come by shortly." Luci nodded.

"It's all going to be just fine," she told Della.

"So," Della said, "do I wanna know why there's blue shit all over your hair?"

Luci reached up, feeling the dried beads of paint that covered her head. She smiled.

"You'll see."

Finally, a doctor arrived. A big, hairy man with glasses straight from the 1970s, and a belly that jiggled a little as he walked. This was definitely *not* Dr. Malloy.

"Hi folks," he said, "I'm Dr. Andrews. Dr. Malloy just got called into a delivery, so I'll be taking over today."

Luci could feel Della shift around uncomfortably next to her.

"So, your chart says you've been experiencing some pain, and had some bleeding?" he asked. Della nodded. "And you're thirty-six weeks, right?" She nodded again. "Mhmm," he said, flipping back and forth through the pages of her chart. He trudged over to the monitor to check the baby's heart rate, his feet dragging a little bit with each step. "Well, everything looks to be in tip-top shape. The baby's heart rate is good, your vitals are fine. I also took a look at the sonogram. I saw in your chart that the baby had a choroid plexus cyst on his brain. As of today, that has completely dissolved."

Luci and Della both let out a collective sigh of relief. That stupid, one-point-two-centimeter-long cyst had been weighing down on them like a house on the Wicked Witch of the East.

"Oh, that is fantastic news," Della said, clasping her hands together.

"So, if everything looks good, do we know why she's in so much pain? And what about the blood?" Luci asked. Della had so quickly stepped into that mom role, where her own well-being would forever come second after the baby's. Dr. Andrews nodded, pushing his glasses up on his nose.

"What we have here is a classic case of Braxton-Hicks contractions. The blood you saw was likely your mucus plug dislodging."

Luci stared blankly ahead. She had no idea what a mucus plug was, but she was pretty sure that just solidified the whole *never having kids* thing. It even *sounded* disgusting.

"I mean, I know I've never done this before, but I've had some mild Braxton-Hicks contractions since I was about twenty-four weeks along. This didn't really feel like that. It was a lot more intense," Della told him, bringing her hands to her belly. Dr. Andrews smiled, a big, fat, smug smile.

"A lot of first-time moms experience the same confusion. Braxton-Hicks aren't really *painful*, per se, but they can get more intense as the pregnancy develops. You are not in active labor," he said.

"Sorry, I just have to ask," Luci heard herself saying, the anger growing inside of her. Maybe it was the feminist inside her, or maybe it was the pent-up sexual energy she hadn't been able to let out. But Della was in pain, and worried. And all Dr. Andrews had to offer was some patronizing sexist bullshit.

"If you don't have ovaries, or a uterus, or a vagina, how can you tell *her* what's painful, and what's not?"

Dr. Andrews' bushy eyebrows raised up high over the rims of his glasses.

"I beg your pardon?"

"Well, you told her the contractions, of her *uterus,* weren't painful. Do you know that from experience? How many kids have you had, Dr. Andrews?" she asked him, taking a step closer.

He didn't say anything. He just swallowed hard, taking a step back from Luci. Finally, he cleared his throat, looking around Luci to Della.

"Mrs. Niles, your, um, your scans looks great. If you experience more intense contractions, or, um, if they come more frequently, please come back. Here's a tip sheet on ways to relieve Braxton-Hicks contraction pain, and, um, take care."

With that, he disappeared out of the room so fast, Luci was pretty sure his feet didn't touch the floor. As soon as he was gone, Della burst into laughter, clutching her enormous belly.

"I think he shit his pants!" she said, wiping tears of laughter from her eyes. "Oh, Luciana Ruiz, you are my hero."

# NINETEEN
*Della*

As they pulled up to her house, Della took a breath. Despite Luci's fierce defense, Dr. Andrews had made her feel like a foolish, uneducated, silly little woman.

She was calmer, understanding that her body was not yet ready to shoot out another human, but the pain was still there, and it was still real. Everything hurt; her body was beginning to feel as if it had expanded to its capacity, ready at any minute to burst at its seams. She had actually searched "pregnant belly buttons" on the internet; she was pretty sure if she breathed out hard enough, hers was going to pop off.

"Ugh," she said, letting Cash reach down and pull her out of the car. Even the simplest things were beginning to feel taxing, and she was in no position to refuse help of any kind. Behind them, Dayton and Luci pulled up in his squad car, and Della smiled as he opened her door, his arm falling naturally around Luci's shoulders as they made their way up the walk.

"How ya feelin', champ?" Dayton asked Della as they got closer, Luci taking her other arm to help lead her up the steps.

"Eh, ya know. Apparently I'm not in pain, so I guess I'm fine," she said sarcastically. Dayton scoffed.

"That guy is an idiot," he said, rushing ahead of them to hold the screen door open.

Inside, Della waddled to the recliner, collapsing into it. Luci appeared next to her, pulling the lever up and propping a pillow up underneath her feet.

Like clockwork, there was a knock on the front door, and Dayton went to answer it. Mrs. Ruiz walked in with a brown bag full of carryout food, and from the looks of it, it was enough to feed an entire party. Cash's eyes lit up with excitement, and Della realized that none of them had eaten in hours. Her little army was so dedicated.

"Okay, so, I stopped and got Smokehouse on the way over," Mrs. Ruiz said, walking back to the kitchen table to dig through the bags. "I grabbed brisket, ribs, and pulled pork, a little of everything. I know you all have to be starving," she said.

"Oh, brisket!" Della said, surprised at her sudden craving.

"Brisket, coming right up," Mrs. Ruiz said, scooping some onto a plate and delivering it to her on her plush throne. "I also looked up some home remedies for Braxton-Hicks contractions. You need tons of water, and to keep your feet up when they become more intense. It also said that you shouldn't do a lot of movement or strenuous things, and—"

"Water and these pillows are good for now, Mrs. R. I'm good, really," Della said. "Please, get some food. Sit down. Relax."

Mrs. Ruiz nodded, scooping some food onto her own plate and joining them for a T.V.-lit dinner in the living room. Della wasn't sure why, but she felt a sense of relief with Mrs. Ruiz there, as if there was someone to look to for answers. Luci and Cash were wonderful caretakers, but when it came to parenting, Della herself was the closest thing to an expert in the vicinity, and that made her stomach flip with anxiety.

Mrs. Ruiz smiled, looking up at her in between bites, checking in on her with every passing moment. Melanie Ruiz was a beautiful woman, tall and slim, blonde hair and blue eyes, with tan skin. It was a running joke since they were kids that Della looked more like her than Luci did; Mr. Ruiz's Cuban roots were extremely dominant. But Luci shared her mother's dark blue eyes, something that Della knew had made her even more irresistible to the boys in high school. And for so long, it had been just the two of them, and Della had always admired their bond, especially after her own mother had passed so suddenly.

"So, listen," Luci said, dabbing at her lips with a napkin, "Dayton and I have a surprise for you. But it's not *quite* ready, so you can't see it yet. So, don't go in the nursery until I give you the clear. Okay?"

Della placed her glass on the coaster next to her, and raised an eyebrow. She'd had a feeling the nursery was going to be a project of Luci's, but she didn't want to ruin the surprise. After the paint specks in her hair, and the obviously-planned day of activities with Cash, she knew *something* was going on. What she wasn't expecting, though, was that Dayton would be her apprentice.

"Okay," she said with a smile.

"Did you catch the Wizards last night, man?" Dayton asked Cash. Cash piped up, his attention turning back to the other humans in the room instead of the freakishly-fit ones on ESPN.

"Hell yeah!" he said. Then, they were on a roll,

talking about the Wizards, the upcoming Capitals season, and just about every other D.C. sports team there was. It had been a long time since sports talk rang through the house, and although she could barely tell the difference between a touchdown and a foul shot, Della had missed the male camaraderie between Cash and Jackson. He'd always had a friend in Jackson; he'd had a man around, someone to look up to, someone to talk to in a way that he never could with Della.

And now, with Dayton here, Della heard that pep in Cash's voice, that familiar feeling of her heart warming, watching two people she cared about bonding in front of her. She'd missed that light in her brother's eyes. Cash was so special; he was going to make an amazing uncle, and she couldn't be more excited that he was going to play a role in her son's life. She loved having him home, but she knew it probably wouldn't last long. He was currently sleeping on the couch in her basement, and she wasn't sure how long this arrangement would last after he graduated. Luci had offered his old room back on multiple occasions, but he always refused, being the gentleman that he was.

And Luci. Luci had been a Godsend for the last sixteen weeks, doing more for Della than she even knew she needed. That was the thing about her best friend. She truly knew her better than she knew herself, and besides Jackson, Della had never really known another love like it.

She watched Dayton and Luci, moving so effortlessly back into their rhythm together, and she caught herself grinning like an idiot. Luci leaned back on the couch, pulling one leg up to her chest and scooting in, as close as she could possibly get to him. His arm dropped off the top of the couch to rest on her shoulders, as he dropped his head to lay a kiss on her forehead before turning back to the television.

Dayton and Luci were starting over again, back in the beginning, exciting, stomach-flipping stages of their relationship. They knew so much about each other, but they were simultaneously getting to know each other on new levels, and the energy surrounding both of them together seemed to be heightened. But they had history together, just like Della and Jackson did. They had stories from their youth, pictures from their senior prom, mementos from their first dates together as teenagers, which they could someday share with their future kids. Luci had never committed to the idea of having children, but Della thought it might someday happen. After all, Luci was a natural caregiver. Although Della knew Luci would be on top of the corporate world someday, leading the way, she could also just as easily see her with a brood of her own, a small army of mini-Lucis, all setting out to conquer.

As she felt a tiny kick to her ribs, Della put her hand to her bump, rubbing it gently. Although her insides were being crushed, she realized that she only had a few more weeks left of being pregnant. Only a few more weeks of being a human vessel, transporting the most precious cargo in the world. And she wondered if she'd ever have a bump like this again.

If she were ever to have more children, it would be with a man other than Jackson. It would be with a man other than the love of her life. She would have to have *sex* with, maybe even *make love* to, another man.

This baby would have half, or maybe even step-siblings, and a step-father. And that man would be helping her raise *Jackson's* child. And she suddenly felt nauseous.

She reached down, using whatever strength was left in her arms to pull the lever of the chair back down.

"I think I'm going to head upstairs, guys," she said. "I'm not feeling so hot."

"Do you need anything?" Luci asked, standing up. "Do you want me to come up with you?"

Della shook her head.

"No, no. I'm okay. Just need some rest, I think," she said. "Goodnight, guys. Thank you for everything."

She brushed her teeth, pulled her hair into a long braid, and sunk down into the covers. She couldn't shake the feeling of this baby being so close to existing in the outside world, only to discover years later that he didn't have a father. She'd have to teach him everything. How to pee standing up, how to shave. *Everything.*

She leaned across her bed, stretching her fingers toward her end table, using whatever energy was left in her tired body. She finally grabbed her phone and clicked through her saved videos until she found it. The video Ben Knoxville had posted of a seventeen-year-old Jackson. She had saved it the night he posted it, knowing it would break her heart in a beautiful way every time she watched it. She smiled at the boy on the screen in front of her, dancing so effortlessly on the middle of the field. Damn, that boy could dance.

She had plenty of videos of him in his older years, too. But this was the one she found herself watching the most. It took her back, way back, to the beginning of Jackson and Della. To where it all started. To the most beautiful times of her life. And all those silly moments she had taken for granted, every date they had gone on as teenagers that she'd almost forgotten about at this point, she dug deep to remember. She'd give anything to be sixteen again, staring down at him on the field, wearing his jersey in the stands. And as another fluttering kick waved through her belly, she felt the tears welling. She was jolted back to reality with a knock on her door. Even though it was just Luci, she really didn't want to be caught mid-weep. She had had enough of the sympathy.

But to her surprise, in walked Mrs. Ruiz.

"You feelin' okay, hon?" she asked, closing the door behind her and leaning on the foot of Della's bed. Della quickly wiped the tears from her cheeks, pulling herself up into a seated position on her bed, which proved to be *quite* the task these days. Her first instinct was to wave it off, smile, blame it on the hormones. But she had a moment of clarity; she realized that this was her only chance to get this weight off of her chest that only a mother could really understand. She looked down at her hands, folded on her bump.

"I don't know how to do this," she said, barely above a whisper.

"Which part, hon?" Mrs. Ruiz asked.

"Raise him alone. He needs his father," she said.

She saw Mrs. Ruiz look down at the ground, then up at the sky, as if she were looking for the right words to say.

"Oh, honey," she sighed. "I know it feels like that. *Believe* me, I know it feels like that."

She sat quietly for a moment, a sad smile coming over her face. Then she went on.

"When they sent Berto back, God, I was so lost. I had no idea what I was doing. And Luci was *so* young, and all I could think about was how she was going to get through life without her dad. He'd never watch her play a single sport, never see her graduate, never dance with her at her wedding. Your mind goes crazy, thinking about all the things your child will miss. Since she was seven years old, her father has been 'raising' her over the phone," she said, using air quotes. "Berto did the best he could, but it's a little hard to raise a child when there's literally an ocean between you. Thank God for technology, Luci can actually *see* him now. But that's no way to bond. But let me tell you what I've learned, honey. I've learned that when you have a child, no matter the circumstances, you figure out how to give them exactly what they need. You figure out how to make their lives full, how to fill their gaps. Even if it's just you. You figure it out. And I promise you something: this baby is so lucky to have you as his mother."

Della sat quietly for a moment, tears now streaming down both of their faces. Della reached out, taking Melanie's hand, letting her words settle. It was true that Mr. Ruiz was still alive, but he'd been forced to be almost as absent from his child's life as Jackson would be. Melanie had essentially raised Luci completely on her own.

And Luci turned out to be one of the best humans on the planet.

"Thank you, Melanie," Della finally whispered. "Can I ask you one more thing?"

Melanie nodded.

"Did you and Mr. Ruiz. . .was it. . . was it hard being apart? I mean, did you ever. . ." she couldn't figure out exactly how to ask what she really wanted to.

"Are you wondering if there was ever a time we wanted to call it quits?" Melanie asked. Della nodded, sheepishly. "Aw, honey, it was hard being apart for so long. And there was a point where we talked about separating." She paused to laugh to herself. "*Emotionally* separate, that is. We were already a few thousand miles apart. And I just missed him. I missed having someone here. So, we tried it for a few months. Each of us went on a few dates, and came to the same conclusion: it would never work with anyone else. And as much as it hurt being away from him, it hurt that much more trying to move on."

Della nodded.

"But, that's not to say I couldn't be happy eventually with someone else. And that's not to say that *you* can't be happy with someone else, someday. I know it seems impossible right now, but don't close yourself off, honey. Just go with the flow."

Della swallowed hard. She couldn't imagine anyone else's arms around her, her lips on anyone else's, making love to anyone else. It made her sick to her stomach. Melanie took her hand.

"You can do this, baby. You'll do it because you have to. Because you'll have this tiny little person who depends on you every day. And letting him down just won't be an option. You'll see."

# TWENTY

*Luci*

Luci wanted to follow her mother upstairs. She wanted to be in on the conversation, take care of Della. But she had a feeling she should let them be, mother to mother.

"Well," Cash said, rising to his feet, "I am *beat*. I'm gonna hit the hay." He motioned to the basement couch with his thumb.

"No, Cash, you've had a crazy day. I'll take the couch. You get a good night's sleep in the bed tonight," Luci told him.

Cash protested out of politeness, but she could see it would be an easy fight. The couch in the basement had been in Jackson's apartment in college, and was about as comfortable as a dorm room bed. "Nonsense, I'm fine, really. Take the bed."

After Cash said goodnight, Dayton leaned in, pulling her closer to him.

"Ya know, I have plenty of room in my bed, if

you'd rather not sleep on that couch," he said, keeping his eyes on the television. She smiled.

"Hmm, I've yet to actually be in your bed," she said. "I've been just about everywhere *else* in your house." He grinned.

"There's a first time for everything. Do you want to head out? We can grab a drink in town and head to my place."

She nodded, hopping up to grab her bag and slide into her shoes. He followed her to the door, bending down to whisper in her ear before opening it.

"Maybe we can pick up where we left off earlier," he said, and she felt herself melting into a puddle on the ground.

They stopped in at Andy's, grabbing a table in the back. He handed her the drink menu, and she ordered a beer. She was usually a wine drinker, but after the day she had, she felt like a beer was in order. He sat back in his seat, and she felt his eyes on her as she looked at the menu, as if she were going to order something else.

"You're not getting anything?" she asked. He shook his head.

"Nah. After a few years on the job, it's hard for me to have anything and drive. I guess I've seen too much. I am your happy DD tonight," he said, flashing that smile. If she were wearing a dress, she'd probably have to check to make sure her panties hadn't dropped to the ground.

"I see," she said, "so you're just trying to get me drunk?" She smiled back at him, and he leaned across the table.

"Never," he said, "I'm nothing but a perfect gentleman." This made her laugh out loud.

"Ha! You must be forgetting about how you had me naked on your kitchen table a few nights ago."

"Shh. . ." he said, bringing a finger to his lips. She covered her mouth, not realizing how loud she'd said it. He chuckled and shook his head.

"You're something, Luciana Catalina," he said. Her eyes shot to him. His using her middle name felt oddly intimate. It just reminded her of everything he had never forgotten. Everything he'd held on to, just like she had.

After two more beers, Dayton paid the bill and stood up from the table. She followed him toward the door as he held it for her, and she could feel his eyes on her again as they walked across the parking lot. Her eyes trailed out across Main Street, and she took in the sight of sundown across her pretty little town. All the other small shops and businesses were closing down now. The water tower with the big green "D" in the distance, the last few people getting their ice cream fix at Jimmy Cone. She did love Dalesville. And even if she didn't want to end up here, it was a part of her.

But as her eyes made their way back down the street, she froze, staring at the street light in front of the parking lot where Jackson died. She darted across the parking lot, standing extra close to it.

Around it were posters, wreaths, a few crosses. Some had Jackson's name on it, some said "R.I.P." She felt a wave of nausea, and it wasn't from the beer. She brought her hand to her mouth, feeling it quiver. His hands landed on her shoulders, pulling her back from it.

"Luci?" he asked. Suddenly, she was overcome by it all. She'd been in Jackson's home, watched him be lowered into his grave, stopped at the cemetery a few times. But nothing had hit her like this. This was the last place her friend was alive. This was where he took his last breath. This was where his life came to a screeching, deafening halt.

"You okay?" he asked. She nodded.

"It's just. . . Della doesn't get her forever. At least not with Jackson. And it's not fair. He was her *everything*, and she doesn't get him back. Ever."

She felt the tears prickling at her eyes again, but this time, she let them go. She didn't try to stop them, or hide them. If she and Dayton were going to give things another try, she'd need to force some of her walls to come back down.

In an instant, his hands were there, pulling her into his hard chest. She laid her head against it, and he stroked her hair, squeezing her tightly to him. But as amazing as it felt to be back in his arms, letting him be her literal shoulder to cry on, she couldn't stop picturing Della.

Luci had almost lost what she presumed to be the love of her life once, and, all dramatics aside, she felt like it almost killed her. She had done a good job of creating the façade of a fulfilled life, and she truly did love her work. But when all was said and done, even if she had her spot as VP with some giant, corner office, she knew in the back of her mind that something would always be missing, and it wasn't something that a random one-night stand would fix.

But she had the chance to fill that gap, she had her Dayton back in between her arms, and she never had to let him go. But Della didn't have that luxury. Jackson didn't want to leave, but he was ripped out from her grasp.

"Luci, Della's going to be okay," he whispered to her. "She's a tough girl. And she has you, and Cash, and I'll be here for her, too. But besides that, and probably most importantly, she'll have that baby."

Luci wiped her eyes, checking her fingertips for signs of dripping mascara. She looked up at him.

"That baby is just as much Jackson's as he is hers," Dayton said. "She's going to make an amazing mother. And despite all the pain she's feeling, that little boy will work miracles on her life. I just know it."

She paused for a moment, taking in what he was saying. Throughout Della's pregnancy, Luci had been concerned about the extra weight—figuratively and literally—that this baby boy would bring down on Della's life. Della would have to feed him, to care for him, to raise him, all on her own. But what Luci hadn't considered was all of the things this baby would *give* to Della. She smiled at Dayton, standing on her tip-toes for a quick kiss. He smiled back at her, wrapping his arms around her shoulders.

"Shall we?" he asked, holding a hand out toward his Tahoe. She nodded.

When they got to Dayton's, Luci surprised herself with how comfortable she felt. She'd only been here one other time, but the closeness between the two of them since then made it feel like a second home to her. Or maybe even a first one, since she technically didn't have a home in Dalesville.

She shook her shoes off at the door, and took the lead inside. As they walked into the living room, he turned to sit on the couch, but she stopped him.

"I think we spent enough time on that couch the last time I was here," she said with a devious smile. He popped back up.

"Alright, then," he said, sliding his hands around her waist, "where would you like to go?"

She pushed back out of his grasp, her expression growing a bit more serious now. Maybe it was the raw emotion that had been eating away at her since she laid eyes on the lamppost, or maybe it was his intense sexual magnitude, or maybe a combination of both. But she needed him, and she needed him *now*.

She took his hands, walking backwards toward

the steps, pulling him in for long, drawn-out kisses along the way. She paused to run up the stairs, skipping a few like a child, then picked back up where she left off once she reached the top. She grabbed hold of his collar, pulling him down to her level, backing up into one of the doors in the hallway.

"That's the bathroom," he mumbled, his lip still between her teeth. She pushed him off and headed toward another door. He paused, smiled, and shook his head.

"Guest room," he said. She threw her hands up in the air.

"For the love of God, I'm about to do it on the goddamn floor!"

He chuckled, reaching around and pulling her into him. He knelt down, scooping her up and carrying her through, of course, the *last* damn door in the hall.

His bedroom was surprisingly big for how small the house was, but it still felt cozy. He didn't have much; just an oak-colored bed with a beige quilt, and a matching dresser. She smiled. It felt like Dayton.

He caught her off-guard as she was taking the room in, spinning her around and pulling her close for another long kiss. She moaned under her breath, a smile forming over her lips. She pushed him down on the bed, and he smiled, throwing his hands up in surrender.

She climbed on top of him, straddling him, reaching down to slowly, seductively pull his shirt off over his head. *God,* his chest was perfect. She put her hands up over her head, letting him know it was his move. He slipped her tank top off, for the second time that day. Only this time, she'd make sure he finished the job. His fingers followed the path of her bra straps, down her shoulders, around her back to the clasp, and she felt a shiver shoot up and down her spine.

She scooted backwards a bit, swiftly undoing his jeans and chucking them onto the floor behind her. She wasted no time, and within an instant, his boxers had disappeared. He flipped her over onto her back now, gently, slowly, agonizingly shimmying her jeans down over her hips, past her knees, and off of her feet.

He reached up, lacing one finger in the string of her thong, and pulled it down. Then she felt herself coming undone again.

He entered her so slowly that she thought she was going to die. But it didn't take long for them to pick up the pace. After a few beautiful motions, she pushed him off of her, flipping herself around, and climbing on top.

His eyes glowed with excitement as she bounced on top of him, his hands exploring every inch of her, his thumb circling her in ways that made her whole body buck.

They moved from his bed, to his dresser, to the window sill, moaning, breathing, calling out each other's names. She tugged on his hair, scratched at his back, arched her own. And this time, they finished in sync. . .in fact, she actually finished *before* him, wrapping her legs around him tight, wishing the moment could last forever.

When they finally unfolded from each other, she rolled onto the opposite side of his bed, the side closest to the window. He scooted in close, reminding her just how much she loved being the little spoon. He tucked one arm under her pillow, and wrapped the other around her waist. He nuzzled her hair, kissing the back of her neck and her shoulder, making her shudder.

"Luci," he whispered.

"Yes?"

"I love you."

She swallowed hard, closing her eyes and

wrapping her arm around his. When she opened her eyes again, she was still there, in his bed, with him wrapped around her. It wasn't a dream, or a nightmare. He was hers again.

"I love you, too."

It didn't take long for him to drift off into a much-needed sleep. He'd worked the night shift the night before, then spent all day with Luci and Della when he should have been sleeping. Tomorrow was his day off, and she'd already planned on sneaking out of bed early to make him a hearty breakfast. He deserved it.

The moon shone so brightly through the window that it lit up the entire room. She smiled, basking in its glow. And just as she closed her eyes, she heard her phone buzzing in the back pocket of her shorts, somewhere on his floor. She slipped out of bed like some sort of a naked ninja, crawling around on the floor till she found it. Oh God, it had to be Della. What if she was in labor?

Just as she was about to pull on her pants, she flipped the phone over to see that it wasn't Della. It was a new email. From Mia.

She inhaled deep before pressing the tiny envelope.

*Luciana,*

*Hope all is well on the East Coast.*

*I wanted to let you know that an old friend of mine, CFO at Hadley Technologies, is going to be posting an Assistant Vice President position at his company at the end of the month. I have already given him your name and resume, in case you're interested.*

*The position's here in Seattle.*

*Let me know if you want me to put in a good*

*word.*
    *Mia*

    She rolled back from her knees to her butt, sitting naked on Dayton's floor. She stared up at him, his face cool and relaxed in his deep sleep. And she wondered how many times she could abandon opportunity before it stayed clear of her for the rest of her life.

# TWENTY-ONE
*Della*

Everyone had warned Della that the last few weeks of her pregnancy would crawl by, like a sloth, or a snail. But somehow, time seemed to be slipping away faster than she could have imagined, and it was starting to freak her out.

Another week had passed, and somehow, she was on the table at her thirty-seven-week appointment. She caught another glimpse of herself in that cursed mirror, and smiled. When she first got pregnant, Jackson had always said he couldn't wait to see how big she got. He'd put his hands on her belly, kneel down and kiss it, before she even had a real bump. He was so ready to be a father.

Before she could slip into a Jackson haze, the door to her room burst open.

"Hi," Luci said, closing it behind her and quickly sitting down in the chair in the corner of the room.

"Hey," Della said with a crooked smile. Ever since Luci had stayed with Dayton the night of Della's hospital trip, she'd gone back and forth between the two houses each night. Della even noticed her packing a duffel bag of things to leave at Dayton's. "So, how was your night?" she asked. Luci rolled her eyes.

"Are you going to ask me that every time I stay at his house?" Luci asked, crossing her arms. Della shrugged and pointed to her crotch.

"It's been almost five months since I've had any action. *Five. Months.* And after the next few weeks, it could be five lifetimes before I see any again. So yeah, I'm probably going to ask you that every time."

Luci chuckled and shook her head. There was a light knock on the door, and Dr. Malloy stepped in. An immediate feeling of relief washed over Della. Considering her run-in with Dr. Andrews, she was internally ecstatic to see Dr. Malloy.

"How are we feelin' today, mama?" she asked, rolling up to Della on her stool. "I'm so sorry I couldn't see you at the hospital. But the cyst is gone, so that's great news!"

"Oh, yes," Della breathed a sigh of relief, "that was amazing news. I've still been having those painful Braxton-Hicks contractions, though."

"Okay, well, you're thirty-seven weeks this week, so we will do a cervix check today," Dr. Malloy said.

"A what check?" Luci asked.

"A cervix check. Go ahead and lie back for me."

Della did as she was told, watching Luci turn to face the wall out of the corner of her eye. She heard the smacking sounds of Dr. Malloy pulling latex gloves on, and she shivered when she scooted the end of her paper gown up.

"Okay, you might feel a little pressure," Dr. Malloy warned, and then, suddenly, she did. She cringed and hissed as Dr. Malloy did the exam, pausing for a moment when it seemed she'd reached all the way up to Della's brain. Jesus, if it hurt this much with two tiny fingers, how in God's name would it feel when a giant bowling ball of a human head was shoving its way out? Della shook her head, avoiding the thought completely.

"Alright," Dr. Malloy said, her hand finally retreating, "you're only about a centimeter dilated. That's pretty common toward these last few weeks, and unfortunately, it doesn't mean much. You could go into labor tonight, or it could be another few weeks. Just hang in there, okay?" Dr. Malloy asked.

Della wondered why it was "unfortunate" that she wasn't near giving birth yet. She supposed that most mothers at this point would make a deal with the devil to give birth totheir child; swollen feet, ankles, fingers, their bodies seemingly bursting at the seams. But Della didn't have that same anticipation. Instead, she needed time to slow down. She needed these last few weeks to come to terms with everything, to prepare herself for actually becoming a mother.

"Here are some pamphlets that will be helpful to you in these last few weeks. This one," she said, pointing to a long list printed on a pink piece of paper, "tells you signs of labor. Our on-call number for the office is there at the bottom. This one," she said, handing her a large folder with a picture of a mother smiling down at her newborn, "is all the hospital information. It has the address, a map, and information on their lactation consultants. You'll probably keep that one on handy when you go in to deliver, so that the consultants can visit you after you give birth. Now, have you selected a pediatrician?"

Della stared blankly at the materials in her hands. Finally, Luci spoke up.

"Ah, I don't think we've gotten quite that far just yet, you know. Lots of other things to prep for," she said with a sweet smile. Dr. Malloy's eyes grew wide, but she smiled nonetheless.

"Right, okay. Well, here's a list of some in this area. If you can, try and decide on one in the next week or so, so that we can call their office after your delivery. Now, if you have any questions before your appointment next week, feel free to call the office. Otherwise, we'll see you next Wednesday."

Della nodded and smiled, and muttered a hushed "thanks," as Dr. Malloy smiled at Luci and stepped out of the room. Luci knelt down to grab Della's maternity dress, and spun back around as Della removed her tissue paper gown to put it back on.

"Holy shit," Della said, still staring ahead.

"I know," Luci said, already knowing that Della was taking a fast turn into Anxiety-ville. "I'll start calling these offices on the way home. We will see if we can get into a few of them tomorrow. Don't worry! We will find the best one. And the nursery is all set up. I'll start washing the baby's clothes this week. Dayton said we could bring the car to the station this week to have the car seat installed. We've got this, Della Bee. You're more prepared than you think."

Della nodded, but she barely heard a word Luci said.

For the next few days, Luci was on a baby-prep rampage. She sent Della to bed, to the recliner, and out to the back patio to relax while she cleaned the house and washed the baby's clothes, in non-scented detergent, of course.

Cash was out getting the car seat installed, and when he got back, Luci had just left to get some grocery shopping done. She was planning on making "at *least* fifteen freezer meals" so that no one would have to cook for the first few days.

Della was more than appreciative of the extra care and attention she was getting, but she was also starting to grow more and more exhausted. She sank into the cushions of the patio bench, feeling like her massive belly would swallow the rest of her body whole if she sank any further. She rubbed it, staring down at the wonder that was the unseen. Her beautiful baby boy. *Jackson's* beautiful baby boy.

Suddenly, a leaf blower started nearby, and she jumped. Seconds later, Dayton strutted by, waving it in a perfect line across her backyard. She smiled as she watched him, walking along, taking care as if it were his own home. He was a good man. As he spun back around to the next row, he caught sight of her, and turned the blower off.

"Sorry," he said, "I didn't wake you, did I?"

"Nope," she said, "I've just been banished out here while Mother Hen does all my work for me."

He laughed.

"Well, you're not supposed to do any work at this point."

"Well, neither are you! Seriously, you don't have to do this. Cash is home now, and I can call a service." He shrugged.

"Nonsense. Besides, this will be the last time we will need to do anything for the season. How are you feeling?" he asked.

"Well, considering I have forty extra pounds of weight attached to me that's crushing my insides, not so bad," she said with a smile.

He walked up onto the patio, and she patted the seat next to her. He sat down, taking in a deep breath.

"So, how are things with Luci?" Della inquired, poking him..

He laughed again.

"What's so funny?"

"Nothing. It's just that you're asking me, when we both know you already know exactly how things are going with me and Luci."

This made her laugh, too. He was, of course, right.

"Well, yeah. I know more details than you probably want me to," she said with a shrug. "But how are *you* doing with it? Are you happy?"

He looked at her, raising an eyebrow. She knew he was probably wondering if she'd been put up to asking him this, but he relented anyway.

"Well, as long as I have her, I'm the happiest I will ever be," he said, so matter-of-factly that it made Della's heart flutter a bit. There's something so beautiful, so fulfilling about knowing that someone *you* love is loved by another person. There's a relief in knowing that they will forever be cared for, that someone else sees all the beauty you see.

"Dayton," she said, reaching out to put her hand on his, "I can tell you, although I'm probably not supposed to, the feeling is mutual. But we both know that woman in there is stubborn, and difficult, and bossy."

Dayton's eyes darted toward her, a look of concern growing in them.

"But we love her for it," Della added, smiling. "I know she wants to be with you as badly as you want to be with her. So please, whatever problems might come down the line in your future, whatever issues arise, just fight for her. Don't let her go."

She paused for a moment, looking down at her bare ring finger. In the last few weeks, her fingers had grown too swollen to get her rings on and off, and it just about killed her.

"Sorry to be so sappy," she said, "but lately I've become a big proponent of second chances." She winked at him. She would give *anything* for a second chance. Dayton didn't say anything, just sat there, holding Della's hand in his. Finally, he leaned over, wrapping her in a long hug, and she flicked a tear from her cheek.

Just as he stood to make his way back to the yard work, he paused when his phone buzzed in his pocket.

"Briggs," he answered, taking a few steps away from the patio. He was silent for a moment, listening to the person on the other end of the line, his eyebrows pulling together.

"Thanks, Captain," he finally said. "We will be there in just a bit."

Della's eyes darted to him. Who was "we?" Where were they going?

Dayton hung the phone up, and turned slowly to face her.

"Della," he said, clearing his throat, "that was my captain. Della, they found him. They found the man that shot Jackson."

# TWENTY-TWO
*Luci*

She scrolled through the list she'd made on her phone while she absent-mindedly pushed the cart down the aisles. While grocery shopping wasn't exactly her favorite pastime, she had to admit, it was relaxing to slow down and take a second to breathe. She'd been running around like a madwoman for the past few days, trying to keep Della cool and confident. Luci had to convince Della that they were ready for this tiny human that was about to flip their world on its axis, all the while trying to convince herself, and it was proving to be a little bit harder than she had imagined.

Her mother had helped her make a pre-baby to-do list: deep clean the whole house, wash all baby clothes, install car seat, pack hospital bag, and last but not least, make a few freezer meals. Luci was an overachiever, so she didn't take "a few" lightly. She'd loaded her Pinterest page with all kinds of frozen soup, stew, and lasagna recipes, and her cart was filling to its brim.

Just as she checked the milk off of her list, her phone buzzed in her hand. And the moment she saw his name flash on her screen, her stomach twisted and turned.

"Hey, you," she said, trying not to sound as giddy as she felt.

"Hey. Where are you?"

"Just finishing up some pre-baby grocery shopping. How about you?"

"I'm on the way down to the police station. Luce, they caught the guy that shot him. They got the guy that shot Jackson. He's in custody," he said, his voice almost cracking.

Luci stopped in the middle of the aisle, clutching a hand to her chest, her heart rate accelerating.

"Oh, my God," she whispered, feeling a wave of intense emotion rush over her. "Does Della know?"

"Yes, she knows. I was with her when I got the call. She could probably use some company. She tried to keep it together while I was there, but I know she was struggling."

"Yeah, of course. I'm just about done here, anyway," she said. "I'll head right home. How did they catch him?"

"Word is that Cora spotted his car at a gas station about twenty miles outside of town. She called the police immediately, and when they showed up, they found a gun in his car that matched the ballistics report from the bullet that killed Jackson."

"Jesus," Luci said. "I can't believe they have him."

"I know, Luce. Finally. Della mentioned that she might want to come down to the station. Let me know if you guys ends up coming down."

"Of course. I'll call you soon," Luci said.

"I love you, Luce," Dayton said, and it almost took her breath away. No matter how many times he said it, she still couldn't believe he was back, saying it again.

"I love you, too," she said.

◊

"Dell?" Luci said, stumbling through the front door with every single grocery bag on her arms. She was a one-trip kind of girl. Two trips were for the weak.

"In here," Della said, her voice quiet, subdued, coming from the kitchen table. When Luci walked in, she was sitting upright, swirling a glass of water around in her hand, staring ahead. When Luci reached her, Della's eyes met hers.

"They got him," she whimpered, then burst into tears. Luci bent down, wrapping her arms around Della, letting her let loose.

"I know, Dell. I know," she said, rubbing her back as she cried, and cried, and cried. Finally, Della collected herself, wiping the last of the tears from her eyes.

"Will you go down there with me?" she finally asked.

"Of course," Luci said, swiping her keys from the table.

When they arrived at the police station, Dayton met them at the door, escorting them through the building to an office on the second floor. As they made their way around, Della's eyes scanned every face on the way, and Luci knew she was trying to catch a glimpse of him.

Dayton offered them a seat across from his desk, where he pulled out a file and set it in front of them. He took a breath, and flipped the folder open. Then they saw his headshot, and Della's spine straightened next to her, as she put a protective hand on her bump.

"This is him?" Della asked. Dayton nodded.

"Timothy Band," he said. "Fifty-two, from Cold Springs, West Virginia. He's got a rap sheet longer than the damn Declaration of Independence," Dayton told her. "He's wanted in West Virginia for assault and battery, and has had a few domestic violence disputes against him, too."

Luci watched Della carefully, trying to gauge her reaction. Della just stared at the bright blue eyes that stared back at her with a demented smile from the photo on the table.

"So, what happens now?" Della finally asked, just as Luci reached for her hand.

"Well, now we get ready for trial. Once it's scheduled, you can be there as much as you'd like," Dayton told her. Then, he stood up, coming around from the desk, and kneeling in front of her. He took both of her hands in his, and looked up into her eyes.

"Della," he said, "I want you to know that I'll be here for you through every step of this. This bastard is going down for life, I promise you that. But whatever you need till this is over, you just let me know. Okay?"

Luci felt her heart swelling. She could feel herself falling harder for Dayton with every word he spoke. He was so passionate, so loyal to the people he loved. It was one of the things she adored most about him.

She couldn't help but wonder, though, what this case brought up for Dayton. Timothy Band's story looked a bit similar to his father's. But at least Timothy was caught. He was done for, locked down, about to pay for what he'd done.

Maybe, someday soon, Mr. Briggs would have the same fate.

# TWENTY-THREE
*Della*

She hadn't slept in three days, ever since she laid eyes on Timothy Band's mugshot.

She had thought about this moment daily since Jackson died; she was ready to feel peace, to feel calm, to feel secure.

But she didn't. She felt alone. She felt panic, uneasiness. And most of all, she felt hatred building in her.

As Della lay in bed, snuggled up in one of Jackson's sweatshirts, she heard her phone buzz on her nightstand.

"Cora?" she asked sleepily.

"Hi, Della," Cora said, her voice shaky.

"Is everything alright?" Della asked. It was past midnight.

"Yes. Well, sort of," Cora said, pausing for a minute. "I suppose you heard that they caught the suspect?"

"I did. Thanks to you," Della said. "I can't thank you enough, Cora."

"It's weird. I thought I'd feel better, but I don't. If it's possible, I feel a little bit worse," Cora said.

Della laid her head back against her headboard. She knew exactly what Cora meant.

"Yeah. I thought I would feel a lot more relief than I feel right now," Della said.

"Why do you think that is?" Cora asked. "How can we not feel better?"

Della thought for a minute, running her thumb across her bottom lip.

"Because Jackson's still dead. And because you still suffered major trauma that night, that will probably stick with you for the rest of your life," Della said. Her answer was blunt, but truthful.

"I hate him," Cora whispered, and Della knew she was crying.

"I know, Cora, I know," Della said. "I hate him, too."

There was another long silence on the phone before Cora finally spoke again.

"Will we get better? Will things get better for us?" she asked, sniffling.

"Yes. They will. I know they will," Della said, lying through her teeth. "But until then, you call me anytime you need. Okay?"

"Thank you, Della. Goodnight," Cora said.

"Goodnight."

As the phone slipped out from her hand and onto the bed, Della pulled her knees up to her belly and sobbed into Jackson's pillow.

Now, she had a face. She had a name, she had someone who she could pin all her pain on, someone who'd caused the worst tragedy of her life.

It was all-consuming. One-too-many times,

she'd pictured herself in the courtroom, hopping over the gate and slamming Timothy's head into the table in front of him. Pregnant belly and all.

◊

The next morning, she lay on the couch, flipping through the channels with a pile of grapes resting on top of her bump.

"How ya doin', Della Bee?" Luci asked, emerging from the kitchen.

"Eh," was all she could muster up.

"How are you feeling about it?" Luci asked. Just as Della switched to another station, something caught her eye, and she switched back.

It was Timothy Band, staring back at her from the screen.

"Local authorities have a suspect in custody from the June murder of a Dalesville man. Timothy Band of West Virginia was apprehended earlier this week at a gas station in Kempsburg. According to reports, Band shot and killed Jackson Niles when Niles attempted to stop him from assaulting a young woman. Police say that Band is being held without bail, and trial is expected to start next month," the reporter said.

Both women stared at the screen, unable to speak for a few minutes. Dayton warned them that it wouldn't be long before the local stations caught wind of the arrest, but it didn't make it any less shocking that they were somewhat prepared for it.

"Dell?" Luci finally spoke up, grabbing for her hand. "You okay?" Della blinked a few times, still staring at the screen.

"I need to see him," she whispered.

"See who?" Luci asked.

"Timothy," Della said. Luci's eyebrows shot up.

"Della, I don't know if —" Luci started to say, but Della was already ungracefully pushing herself up from the couch.

"I have to see him," she said again, heading for the front door.

"Okay," Luci said, following her out.

On the way to the county jail, Luci called Dayton to let him know they were on the way there. He was surprised, but he didn't try to stop them. He couldn't guarantee that Della would be able to get in to see Timothy, but he promised to meet them there and that he'd do his best.

When they arrived, Dayton met them at the door, guiding them through the long corridors of the station again.

They finally reached the back of the building, and stopped at a thick metal door, guarded by two officers. Dayton spoke to them for a minute. One of the guards looked around Dayton to Della, his eyes falling to her bump. He nodded slowly, then unlocked the big door behind him. Della swallowed nervously as Dayton made his way back to them.

"Okay, they are going to let us in. But only for a few minutes," he whispered. But Della shook her head.

She didn't quite know what she was going to say to Timothy Band. But she knew she needed to say it alone.

"I need to go by myself," she said. Dayton and Luci stared at her wide-eyed in disbelief.

"Della Bee," Luci said.

"I don't know if that's such a good idea, Dell," Dayton said. But she stood her ground.

"I'm going alone," she said, a little louder.

Finally, Luci and Dayton nodded in unison, both knowing they would never quite understand the place

Della was in. The guard held his hand out, leading her through the door. At the end of another hall, he spoke to another guard, who then left to bring Timothy to the visitation room.

The guard led Della to a cubicle, with a phone and a thick layer of glass in front of her, just like in the movies. She swallowed.

In a moment, she was going to be face-to-face with him. Her palms began to sweat, but she felt inexplicably steady. She was ready for this.

After another minute or two, she heard the clanking of handcuffs, and then, he was there.

The same striking blue eyes from the mugshot, the same damn smug look on his face.

"Hello," he said, through his phone as he took a seat on the other side of the glass. His voice sent a shiver down her spine. She narrowed her eyes at him, violent scenarios flying through her head like a Stephen King movie reel.

God, she wanted this man to feel excruciating pain. She wanted him to die. Slowly and painfully.

And then she realized, *that* was just why she was here. Because the hate was heavy. It was crushing, debilitating.

"My name is Della. You killed my husband," she said, calm and steady. His eyebrows shot up on his face.

"I thought months ago that you took my life away. I thought you had power, I thought what you did ended me," she went on.

She had no idea why it was so easy to speak to him, but the words felt like they were being pulled out of her. She reached into her purse and pulled out her phone, scrolling through her photos.

"But I was wrong. You didn't end me. Because Jackson," she said, slapping a photo of him against the glass, "he gave me life. This life." She pointed down to her bump, watching as his eyes trailed down to it.

"He gave me everything I've ever needed. And you? Well, your life ended as you knew it the day you took his."

She watched as he swallowed. He didn't speak a word; he just stared ahead at her through the glass.

"Timothy, I'm not going to pray for you, I'm not going to sit here and tell you I forgive you. Because I'd be lying. If I'm being honest, I don't give a rat's ass about what happens to you, or your soul, if you even have one.

"I came here today for myself, and for my son. Because I won't bring this baby into the world holding all this hate in my heart for you. I'm not here to forgive you. But I'm here to tell you that you will no longer occupy a space in my mind. You'll no longer haunt me. Because I'm stronger. Jackson was stronger."

She slammed the phone back on the receiver, popping up from the chair and walking back to the guard, who, thankfully, read her purposeful steps and opened the door without asking more. She didn't even wait to see if Timothy had a word to say edgewise. She didn't care if he was going to say something smug and infuriating, or apologetic and remorseful. She didn't care at all.

When she reached Luci and Dayton again, she could tell they were both nervous wrecks. They each took a hand, waiting cautiously for her to speak.

"Well," Della said, as they made their way back to the car, "that's it. That's enough. That's the last bit of hate Timothy Band will drag out of me."

Luci kissed her temple as Dayton squeezed her hand.

"I'm so proud of you, Della Bee," Luci whispered.

# TWENTY-FOUR
*Luci*

As Luci chopped chicken that evening, she couldn't help but picture him. His face was ingrained in her brain. Timothy Band. Fucking bastard.

She wished more than anything she could have gone in with Della. Just to look him in the eye. To stare him down. Let him know he was done for. But she had to respect Della's wishes. And she knew Della said enough to him for the both of him.

Just as she dumped the chicken into a bowl, her phone buzzed on the counter. She smiled when his name flashed on the screen.

"Hey, you," she said, adding a dollop of mayonnaise to the bowl.

"Hello, beautiful," he said, his voice sounding tired, but happy.

"What are you up to?" she asked.

"Just got off of my shift. Listen, are you busy tonight? I was thinking maybe I could take you out, seeing as we may not have many baby-free evenings left."

His words made her pause mid-stir. She hadn't given much thought to how much of her own time the baby might take. Della had joked about not seeing much action herself after the baby was born, but Luci hadn't thought about the fact that she might not, either.

Luci shook her head. As good as the sex was with Dayton, there was no *way* she'd give that up. She'd sneak over in the middle of the night. She'd risk losing those precious hours of sleep.

The few times they'd made love since she'd been back in Dalesville, it was gloriously intense. He stared into her eyes, grasping her body tight, like he was afraid she was going to slip away again. No *way* was she going without him, now that she had him back.

"Yeah, that would be great," she said with a smile. She knew exactly what she had planned for their evening.

"Great. How does seven work?"

"It works perfect."

As she put the bowl of chicken salad into the fridge, Cash came down the steps.

"Has she been resting?" she asked him,

"Eh, somewhat. She's been watching *Golden Girls* reruns, but she's also been trying to help me with the bathrooms. Don't worry, I forced her back to the couch."

"Nice work," Luci said with a smile.

"I can hear you two jabbering on about me, ya know," Della said, waddling her way down the steps, one hand on the railing, and one on her belly. Luci giggled.

"How are you feeling?" she asked Della once she made it to the kitchen.

"Bored. Can we do something fun tonight?" she asked. Luci felt a pang to her heart.

"Oh, um, yeah, of course. I just need to let Dayton know..."

"Let Dayton know what? Is he your keeper now?" Della said with a smile. Luci rolled her eyes.

"No. We were just planning on having dinner, but I can see him tomorrow."

"No, no, no. Don't change your booty call plans on my account. Go ahead, don't worry about little old me. I'll be fine, all by my lonesome... " Della said, wiping a pretend tear from her eyes and sniffling.

"Hey, what am I, chopped liver?" Cash said. "I'll be here."

"Oh, yeah. See? I don't need you Luce," Della said, sticking her tongue out.

Before Dayton picked her up, Luci put on a pot of her mother's chicken noodle soup. The fall air was crisp now, and she felt like she couldn't leave Della and Cash to fend for themselves, as if they were helpless children.

As she stirred the pot for the last time, Dayton knocked on the door. Cash took the ladle from her hand.

"*Go,*" he said. "Get out. You are officially off duty."

She laughed.

"Alright, you two. I'll probably be out late. I'll text you if I end up staying there."

"Yeah, yeah. Go on," Della said, waving her off with a smile.

"You look amazing," Dayton said, taking her hand as he helped her out of his car. They were at Regal's, the only somewhat high-end restaurant in Dalesville. When they walked in, the hostess, who Luci figured couldn't be more than eighteen or nineteen, flashed her pearly-white smile at Dayton.

"Just two tonight?" she asked, her long, mascara-clad eyelashes batting in his direction.

"Yep," he said, putting his hand on the small of Luci's back. She watched as the young girl's shoulders slumped slightly, as if she were accepting defeat after realizing Luci wasn't his sister or his cousin.

Luci smiled to herself as she thanked the girl. She actually found it to be a compliment on her taste in men; it was no arguable matter that Dayton was devilishly handsome. He had the boyish smile, but the stubble and squared jaw of a man.

As they took their seat at a cozy booth near the back of the restaurant, he reached across the table, taking her hands in his.

"It's been a while since we've been here together, huh?" he asked, letting his thumbs stroke the back of her hand.

"It has. I missed going on dates with you," she said, looking down at their hands.

"Then let's not stop going on them," he said.

She felt her stomach knotting up inside of her. With every word he spoke, Mia's email weighed on her mind even heavier. She kept herself preoccupied with all things baby, and she hadn't spoken a word about the email to Della or to Dayton, but she'd thought about it every day since she opened it. She'd have to get back to Mia eventually with a decision, and it had to be soon.

"You okay?" he asked, sensing the change in her mood. She quickly gave him a reassuring smile, squeezing his hand. He smiled back just as their waiter came to take their orders.

They finished up, she practically licking her pasta bowl clean while he patted his stomach after inhaling his filet mignon. Dayton paid the bill, standing up to hold his hand out for her. As they made their way across the parking lot, his arm around her shoulders, he leaned down to kiss her shoulder. She shivered.

"So, where to next?" he asked. "Do you want to come back to my place?"

She paused for a moment, a major sense of deja vu coming over her as the breeze blew through her thick curls. She'd been here before, walking through this old parking lot, him wrapped around her. She smiled.

"How about Beecher Farm?" she asked, a devious smile coming over her face. His lips curled into a half-smile, and he raised his eyebrows at her.

"Are you serious?" he asked. They hadn't been to Beecher Farm since they were eighteen, sneaking out of their parents' houses to hook up on top of one of the rolling hills. She raised her eyebrow back at him, and he got the hint. "Alright."

"Tell me something, how bad is it if a cop trespasses?" she asked as he started the engine of his Tahoe. He laughed.

"Well, luckily for me, the Beechers have started going down to Florida every fall and winter. So we should be in the clear."

When they finally reached the crest of their favorite hill, the one with the best view of all of Dalesville—including the farm's long driveway, so they could be on the lookout for anyone approaching—Dayton turned off the engine and sat back in his seat. If she didn't know any better, she'd think he was actually a little nervous, and it made her smile to herself.

"I don't have the old truck anymore, so we don't exactly have the best makeshift bed now," he said.

"Hmm," she said, unbuckling. "I think we can make it work."

She climbed on top of him in the driver's seat, reaching down to pull the lever and lay it completely back.

"Whoa!" he said, throwing his hands up in the air. She laughed, leaning down to kiss him, hard. The kisses started out light, like two teenagers. And then they got heavy, like two people who'd been apart for far too long. Before she knew it, she was pulling her dress up, and he was inside of her. And they were making love on the farm, like they'd done all those years ago.

When they finished, he wrapped his coat around her and opened his sunroof so that they could look up at the stars. He laid a trail of kisses from behind her ear, to her jaw, to her neck, and she wriggled under his lips.

"Luci?" he asked. She looked up at him. "I've been thinking a lot about you and I. And I think we should talk about it. I don't want this to end."

"You don't want what to end?" she asked. "Car sex?" she grinned. But he didn't smile back.

"No. Us. I'm just so thankful I have you back. And I've been thinking a lot about Della and Jackson, and what you said about them not getting another chance... and I just don't want to miss ours."

She swallowed hard, pulling his coat around her shoulders more tightly. She knew they needed to have this discussion, and a few days ago, it would have been so easy. She wanted him, and that was that. He was here, Della was here, soon the baby would be here. So it made sense for Luci to be here, too. End of story. No complications.

But now, Mia's name was flashing through her mind. And Seattle. And the life she created for herself. The life she had *loved.* Before, he was the only thing missing. But his life was here in Dalesville. How could she start something up, how could she let herself fall back in love with him fully, knowing she might leave him, the way he had left her?

"Luci?" he asked, nudging her gently with his shoulder.

"I. . ." she started to say.

"What is it?" he asked, pulling the seat back up into its normal position. She climbed off of him and back to her own seat, pulling her feet up onto it and clutching her knees to her chest.

"It's just that I don't know what I want, or where I will be. . .and Della, and the baby. . . there's just so many unknowns. Maybe we can just go slow?"

She watched as his whole body tensed, turning to face the steering wheel. His brow furrowed.

"I don't understand. A few days ago we were talking about never leaving each other again. What's going on?" he asked.

"I. . ." she started to say, but he cut her off.

"Is it my dad?" he asked.

"Oh, God, no," she said, reaching a hand out to touch his shoulder, but pulling it back instantly.

"Then, what could it possibly be? Please, tell me. We can work on whatever it is,"

She froze. They couldn't *work* on three thousand miles. But as her brain stumbled on the right words, they were interrupted by her phone vibrating in the cup holder. She lunged for it.

"Cash?" she asked.

"It's Della. She's in labor."

# TWENTY-FIVE
*Della*

Holy *shit,* this hurt like a bitch.

She and Cash had been playing an intense game of Uno when she felt a sharp pain in her abdomen. She had jumped, putting her hand on her belly. He raised an eyebrow.

"You okay?" he asked. She nodded, breathing in slowly through pursed lips.

"It's the Braxton-Hicks again," she said.

"Come *on,*" Cash said, smacking his hand on top of the draw pile. "Another damn Draw Four? How many of those are you hoarding?"

Then she felt another pain. She couldn't describe it; it almost felt like all of her insides were being squeezed by a giant hand. As if they were contracting. Wait. . .oh.

She shook her head, telling herself silently that it was just more of the Braxton-Hicks. But her eyes darted toward the clock on the wall. She breathed in slowly again, laying down another card.

Five minutes later, she felt another squeeze. Then four-and-a-half minutes later, she felt another. Maybe she just needed to pee.

She stood up from the couch, and froze as what felt like the freaking Nile poured out of her body. But it wasn't pee. She'd heard that some women's water never even broke when they went into labor. Or, some women's water broke in the shower, so they never knew. Guess she was one of the lucky ones who needed a full change of clothes.

"Oh, shit," she said, her eyes lowering down to the growing wet spot forming between her legs.

"Holy shit," Cash said, jumping to his feet. "Wh-wha-what do we do? What do I do? What do you need?"

She could practically see the beads of sweat forming on his brow already.

"Calm down. I'm going to go change my clothes. You call Luci. And then you take me to the hospital."

Her lifetime of being a big sister had helped her perfect the "calm, cool, and collected" act. After all, she'd had Cash's eyes watching her all these years, gauging her reaction to every dire situation in their lives. And even now, in her time of need, she'd put on the act for him.

But on the way to the hospital, she felt her stomach spinning, and it had nothing to do with the pregnancy. In mere hours, she'd be a mom. She'd meet her son. Her and Jackson's son.


"How are we feeling today, Mrs. Niles?" her nurse said, walking into the room and flipping her fire-red ponytail over one shoulder.

"Um, pretty good, I guess. Definitely feeling those—oh, oh, ow," she said, pausing for a minute and squeezing her eyes shut. "Oh, whoa, sorry. Definitely feeling those contractions."

Cash stood at the side of her bed, anxiously rocking back and forth on his feet, heel-to-toe and back again.

"I know, they are definitely getting stronger, and coming closer together. Have you thought about whether or not you'd like an epidural?" the nurse asked.

"Hell, yes," Della said with a snort. "I'm not tough like those drug-free women. I'm a big ol' wimp. Give me the drugs." The nurse laughed.

"Okay, no problem," she said. "I'll just go put the order in and the anesthesiologist should be here within the hour."

Della's eyes shot up.

"Within the *hour?*" she asked. "I've got to be getting pretty far along, right? Are we sure he won't miss the window? I read that if I get past a certain point. . . what was it, four centimeters, I think—I can't get the epidural. And I really, *really* need the epidural."

"Actually, we administer them all the way up until eight centimeters in this hospital," the nurse said. "And right now, you're only about three centimeters dilated. The doctors typically like to wait until you're four or five centimeters dilated, so the timing should be perfect."

Della nodded slowly, laying back in her bed. Moments later, Luci burst through the door.

"Hey, where's your boo?" Della asked, lifting her head up from the pillow.

"He's um, he's out in the waiting room. I told him he could leave, but he said he was staying. For Jackson," Luci said, still catching her breath. Della nodded.

"Is it okay if I um. . . " Cash started to say, pointing to the door.

"Go," Della said. "Hang with Dayton. Della will keep you updated." Cash nodded, the color returning to his pale face when he realized he was now relieved of birthing partner duties. He leaned down to kiss Della on her forehead.

"You are going to be the best mom in the world," he whispered to her. Della felt tears stinging at the back of her eyes. "I can't wait to meet my nephew!" he added, pointing to Della as he made his way out of the room.

"Is everything okay?" Della asked, as Luci pulled the big blue chair in the corner of the room closer to the bed, making herself more comfortable. "Between you and Dayton, I mean."

"Yes," Luci said, waving her hand. "We're fine. Can we concentrate on you having this baby, please?"

"Hate to break it to you, but after a careful inspection of my hoo-ha, the nurse says I'm only three centimeters dilated. It could be a while. Feel free to distract me," Della said.

Luci sighed, and Della knew there was more weighing on her than she was letting on.

"I guess I just don't know what I want, long-term. And—"

She paused as Della pushed herself up on her elbows, eyes squeezed shut, breathing in through the sharp, twisting, contracting pain. She flopped back on the bed as the contraction ended, giving her temporary relief.

Holy *shit*. This was ridiculous. Anxiety was growing inside of her in anticipation of the next one. And just when she thought she'd gotten the new timing down, thirty seconds or so would drop off of the intervals, and another one would sneak up on her.

"You okay, Della Bee? What can I get you?"

"Some damn drugs," Della said, finally catching

her breath after another intense one. She could feel sweat forming on her hairline, coming in thicker with each contraction.

The nurse trotted back in after another half an hour.

"Are you ready for another cervix check?" she asked, pulling on a latex glove and waiting for Della's approval to violate her. "You're pushing five centimeters now," she said, snapping the gloves off her hands and dumping them into the waste bin before pumping her hands full of sanitizer. "The anesthesiologist is seeing his last patient before you. He should be in any minute."

Della nodded, breathing through pursed lips, the smile on her face when Luci walked in long gone. She didn't think anything could make her smile again.

After another five minutes, the anesthesiologist sauntered into the room, ready for action. He never smiled, and was quick and short in his direction.

"Sit on up there, and let your feet hang off the side of the bed. Now just go ahead and concentrate on your friend, there," he said. Luci positioned herself directly in front of Della on her chair. Della shivered as he opened the side of her gown, exposing her entire backside to the world—okay, it was only to the two nurses in the room, but it felt like a lot more. His fingers trailed down her spine, and then she felt the cool sensation of iodine solution spreading across her skin. She swallowed. She knew this was going to help her, but she also knew just *how* these things entered her bloodstream.

"You're going to feel *so* much better after this, Della Bee," Luci said, resisting the urge to take Della's hand. That was against epidural rules.

"Okay, now, you're going to feel a small pinch," the anesthesiologist said, fiddling with some object behind her back. Judging by the size of Luci's eyes, Della guessed that object was the infinitely long needle about to penetrate her body in mere moments. But as everyone in the room paused for one more intense contraction, Della clutched the sheets and gritted her teeth.

"I am so ready," she said. She just needed the damn juice.

"So, as I was saying, you'll feel a small pinch first, then a big one," he said. "And, here we go."

She felt the needle going in, then—*DAMN*—the small pinch. Then *HOLY FUCKING SHIT,* the *big* pinch. It was more than a pinch; it was more like a small electrical shock. A small yelp escaped her lips, and she bit down on her bottom one to keep herself quiet. Tears were forming in her eyes, and she felt like the biggest baby. She hadn't cried due to physical pain in years.

"Okay," the anesthesiologist said, packing up all the fun things he'd brought with him, "all seems to have gone well. You can press this button when you're really feeling the pain, and it will deliver another dose to you." She nodded.

"Thank you," Luci said for Della, knowing she didn't exactly have the mental capacity to formulate words yet. Luci and one of the nurses helped Della scoot back on the bed. Luci fluffed her pillows, and the nurse tucked the blanket in all around her.

Before she knew it, another damn contraction was taking over her whole body.

But after another five minutes, all she could feel were small tingles all around her midsection, and down to her legs.

"Am I having a contraction?" she asked, lifting her head slowly. The nurse glanced over at one of the million blinking machines next to her bed.

"It looks like it, yep. It looks like that epidural

has finally kicked in!" the nurse said with a big smile.

"Thank *God,*" Luci said, letting herself relax a little now. "I hate seeing you in this much pain."

"Eh, it's nothin,'" Della said, lying back and waving her hand. Luci laughed.

"It's nothin' now, because you're on drugs," she said. Della just shrugged, eyes closed. And then, she actually drifted off to sleep in the middle of labor.

She awoke some time later to someone gently rubbing her shoulder. It was Luci.

"Hey, Della Bee, they want to do another cervix check," she said. Della nodded, pulling herself up into a sitting position. Except that she couldn't exactly move her lower half, a moment of panic setting in. She'd almost forgotten about the enormous needle that had numbed her whole body. The enormous, magical needle that took away all the pain.

A nurse walked into the room, pulling a latex glove from a box that was hanging on the wall. But Della didn't recognize her.

"I'm Cindy, your new nurse," she said, sliding the glove down her heand.

"What happened to the other ones?" Della asked.

"Well, their shifts ended. You've been in labor for about thirteen hours now," Cindy said, making her way toward Della and pulling the blankets up over her knees. Another nurse came in to help position her legs while Cindy's fingers felt their way through Della. She knew that normally she'd be squirming uncomfortably. But right now, someone could pitch a tent up there and she swore she'd never know.

"Well, Mrs. Niles," Cindy said, retreating and removing the gloves, "you are at ten centimeters. It appears the baby has dropped and is making his way down the birth canal. We're going to go grab Dr. Malloy. It's time to start pushing."

Della looked to Luci, sheer panic in her eyes. She could hear her heart pounding in her ears. This was it. Suddenly, she felt the pain coming back again. They had told her that at a certain point, they'd cut back on the epidural so she could gain a little more control of her body in time to push. Gaining control also meant feeling the searing pain through her body.

And it meant that she'd be pushing. And it meant that soon, her son would be here, whether she was ready for it or not.

Luci's eyes were wide and full of excitement. Della's were now filling with tears.

"Hey, hey, hey," Luci said, running her hand across Della's clammy forehead as the tears streamed down her face. "What is it, Della Bee? Are you hurting?"

Della lay back on the bed, staring up at the ceiling. This was all wrong. He wasn't here, and he wasn't going to be here. And that hurt more than any damn contraction.

"He's supposed to be here for this. He's supposed to wipe my forehead and hold my legs, and tell me how great I'm doing. He's supposed to cut the cord and tell me how beautiful the baby is when he sees him," she said, breaking into a low sob.

Luci wrapped her arms around Della tight.

"You listen to me, Della Niles. That man is here. Do you hear me? Do you really think he'd miss this? He is *here.* Right here, next to you, watching over you and this baby. Let's make him proud, eh?" Luci whispered.

Della heard her words, and though any other time she'd like to wallow in her sorrows a little longer, the human trying to make its way from her body was a bit distracting. Moments later, Dr. Malloy walked into the room with Cindy and another nurse.

"How are we feeling today, mama?" she asked, as a nurse aid tied a long, periwinkle-colored gown on her.

"Well, you know, I've felt better," Della said, wiping her eyes and forcing a smile.

"Okay, here's how this is going to work. When you feel a contraction coming on, I want you to tell us. We will help you by holding your legs, and you'll push for a count of ten," Dr. Malloy told her, rolling up toward Della's bed on a stool. Della nodded, a mix of emotion, pain, and anxiety swirling around in her body parts that were now starting to come back to life.

Suddenly, she felt a tingle, that turned into a hard pinch.

"One's coming," she said. The nurses moved swiftly, one on each side of her, hooking their legs under her knees and pulling them toward her enormous belly. Dr. Malloy began counting.

"Push, sweetie," Cindy said.

"You got this, Della," Luci told her. At ten, they lowered her legs and she took a breath. *That* was not fun. When she finally caught her breath, she turned to Luci to speak. But her breath was stolen by the onset of another contraction. The cycle continued for another fifteen minutes.

"Okay, let's make this one a big one, now, okay? Ready, go!" Dr. Malloy said, sounding a bit like an obnoxious cheerleading coach.

Della squeezed and pushed as hard as she could, not fully sure if she was even engaging the right muscles. The epidural had definitely worn off a bit, but some parts of her were still numb. At one point, she was pretty sure she was just squeezing her eyes, but no other part of her was working to expel a child.

And then suddenly, she heard some sort of wet, gurgling, ungodly sound. Her eyes popped open as the nurses all stood at attention for a brief moment, before jumping to grab towels and pads and wipes.

Della turned to Luci slowly.

"Did I. . .did I just *shit* myself?" she asked. Luci stared at her, eyes as wide as saucers, lips pursed together. First, she shook her head no. But they both knew she couldn't lie. Her head shake slowly morphed into a nod. Della brought her hand to her mouth, mortified. And then, she burst into a fit of laughter. After a moment, Luci joined her, collapsing into the chair beside Della's bed.

"Well, it's a party now!" Della finally said, wiping the tears of laughter from her eyes. The nurses just smiled as they wiped Della's bottom like she was an infant, replacing her sheets and the pads on the bed in record time, with little-to-no disturbance to Della.

She decided in that moment that nurses weren't human; they were some sort of breed of alien, or superhuman, that weren't bothered by the most vile sounds, sights, and smells a human body could produce. Maybe they were angels. Yep, living, breathing angels.

"Okay," Dr. Malloy said, glancing up at the machine, "it looks like you have another one coming. Let's bear down now." She rolled back between Della's legs, and Della braced herself. Luci put her hands on Della's shoulders, and the nurses kept her legs pinned in their positions, basically folding her in half as she pushed. She could hear herself screaming, yelling, cursing, but it felt like she was hearing herself from a football field away.

"Della, the baby is crowning now. I need one more big push," Dr. Malloy said.

# TWENTY-SIX
*Luci*

Holy shit. Holy. Fucking. Shit. Luci could see hair. Black, thick, beautiful, human hair. She stood, mouth gaping as Dr. Malloy coached Della through another push, and more of the baby appeared. Luci reached up, squeezing Della's hand. She forgot for a moment that she was currently staring into the abyss that was her best friend's vagina. Or, what *used* to be her vagina, at least.

Another push, and his whole face was visible. Before Luci could realize what was happening, she heard herself sobbing.

"Della Bee, he's gorgeous!" she managed to cry out, her voice shaky.

"Okay, one more push, Della, one more!" Dr. Malloy called out, and Luci took her position at Della's side once more. She let Della squeeze her hand as hard as she needed to. Once, twice, and then, he was born. Fully, and completely born.

His whole body was a purplish-grayish color,

and he was covered in fluids that Luci would rather not think about. In fact, she didn't think about them. All she could concentrate on was his face, puffy, but perfect, his shrill cry, his beautiful little body.

"Della! You did it! He's so, so beautiful!" Luci cried again, wiping the tears from her eyes. Della laid eyes on her son as the doctor pulled him up into her line of view, and she burst into tears.

"Oh, my sweet baby," she said, lying her head back against the pillow in what Luci could see was relief.

"Do you want to cut the cord?" Dr. Malloy asked. Luci looked from Dr. Malloy to the nurse, to Della before she realized that Dr. Malloy was asking *her*. Luci looked to Della. This should have been Jackson. He should have been here, jumping up and down, running down the halls, like Luci knew he would have been.

But Della nodded, and for the first time in hours, she smiled. Luci took a deep breath, and grabbed the scissors from Dr. Malloy. She cut through the cord, surprised at how spongy it felt.

She stepped back for a moment, watching as Dr. Malloy stood, bringing the baby to Della's bare chest.

And she watched the exact moment when her best friend became a mom.

It was so natural, so effortless for Della, the way she knew just how to hold him, how she shushed him from crying, how she kissed his tiny, wrinkled fingers. Luci leaned back, clasping her hands in front of her mouth, saying a quick prayer that Della would always be as happy as she was in this moment.

Everyone in the room sat still for a few moments, letting mother get to know son, leaving his first few moments of life to be peaceful. Finally, Cindy spoke up.

"He's beautiful," she said. "Do you mind if we

clean him up now?" she asked. Della nodded slowly, and Luci could see just how badly she didn't want to hand him off, even to go four feet across the room.

Within minutes, Cindy returned him to Della, letting her reap the rewards of all she had been through.

"Do we have a name yet?" Cindy asked. Luci looked up from the baby's face to Della. This entire pregnancy, she'd never once heard Della talk about names, nor had she asked. In the madness of trying to get through it without Jackson, she hadn't even thought about it.

"Yes," Della said, to Luci's surprise. "His name is Jax Luco Niles."

Luci felt her heart drop.

Della turned to look at her. "He's named after his father, and his godmother."

Luci gasped, tears spilling from her eyes.

"Oh, Della Bee," she whispered.

After a few more minutes of necessary snuggling, another woman walked into the room.

"This is Nancy, our lactation specialist here. Are you interested in breastfeeding?" Cindy asked. Della nodded.

"Yes, I definitely want to try."

"Alrighty, let's get started," Nancy said. Luci stood back awkwardly as Nancy made herself comfortable at Della's bedside, handling her boobs as if they were pizza dough. Luci cringed as Nancy folded and poked and prodded and squeezed at them, trying to make them fit into the infinitely small mouth of a newborn.

"Look at that," Nancy said, standing back to admire her work. "He's a pro already. *That* is a beautiful latch."

Della squealed with delight as she stared down at Jax suckling away.

"Luci! Are you seeing this? He's *doing* it!" she cried. "I'm feeding my kid with my *body!*" Luci nodded excitedly, not quite sure how to respond. It actually was kind of cool.

After his first feeding, Della turned to Luci.

"So," she said, "do you want to hold your godson?" she asked.

Luci nodded nervously. She walked to the corner of the room and pumped her hands full of hand sanitizer before sitting down on the bed. Della handed him off as if he were made of glass. Luci put her hands right where Della's had been, careful to support his head. He was wrapped in a tight swaddle, like a little baby burrito. Luci sighed as she stared down at him.

His face was still a little swollen from his, uh, journey, but he really was a pretty baby. His skin was glowing and soft, a perfect mixture of Della and Jackson's. His hair was thick and black under his tiny blue knit hat, and she couldn't get over how small every part of him was. She was definitely in love.

"When you're done swooning," Della said, "I guess we should get my brother. And Dayton, if he's out there still."

Luci nodded slowly, not wanting to give Jax up and face the very grown man who was undoubtedly waiting for her in the waiting room. But she sighed, kissed Jax's head, and handed him back to his mama.

As Luci walked through the entry to the waiting room, Cash practically sprung from his chair.

"How is she? Is he here? Is everything okay?" he said, bounding toward Luci and grabbing her shoulders.

Dayton stood up slowly from his chair, waiting for the answers, and probably trying to get a gauge on Luci's mood toward him. Luci looked back to Cash, and smiled.

"She's fine. And he's here. Your nephew is here," she said. Cash thrust a fist into the air before bending down to pick up Luci and swing her around.

"*Yes!*" he screamed, making the few other people in the room all turn their heads. But Luci didn't care. After all the bad this year, after all the heartache, she was going to let this overwhelming feeling of love and calm surround her as long as it could.

"Let's go back and see him," she said, taking Cash's hand. She looked to Dayton. "Della wants you to come, too."

He raised an eyebrow at her, clearly waiting for her to add something along the lines of, "and so do I." But she didn't.

As they entered Della's room, Luci stood back, leaning against the wall. She watched as Cash charged the bed, his eyes filling with both wonderment and tears. Suddenly remembering himself, he ran to the dispenser on the wall, pumping his hands full of sanitizer.

"Uncle Cash, this is your nephew, Jax Luco Niles," Della said. Cash looked from Della to Luci, then to the beautiful baby in front of him.

"Oh, my God! He's *amazing!*" Cash said, leaning down to kiss Della's head. "You *made* this! Look how small everything is. I could hold him in my hand!" Della laughed.

"Well, do you want to?" she asked. Cash nodded like a kid waiting for ice cream. Luci watched how he handled Jax, gently and naturally, just like Della. It must be a genetic thing. As Cash swayed around the room, humming a song and staring down at the little boy, Dayton made his way to Della's bedside. He knelt down to kiss her cheek and pulled up a chair, taking her hand in his.

"You did great, Dell," he said. She smiled, and Luci couldn't help but feel an overwhelming sense of warmth.

"I can't believe you stayed here all this time!" Della said. "You could have left and come back."

Dayton smiled and shook his head.

"No way. Jackson would have killed me if I left you," he said. She smiled a sad, sincere smile. "I'm really proud of you, Della. That is a beautiful baby. And I know Jackson is proud of you, too."

Luci watched as Della squeezed his hand again, resting her head on Dayton's shoulder for a brief moment.

"Do you want to hold him?" she asked.

Luci perked up. She was currently having enough of a challenge trying to find things that were wrong with Dayton, so she could make it easy to leave. Watching him hold a baby was certainly not going to help her efforts to make him less irresistible.

Cash made his way across the room to Dayton. Luci braced herself for an awkward hand-off, but it never came. He slipped his large hand under Jax's head, cradling him with the other arm and resting him against his chest. He made clicking noises with his mouth as he stared down at the tiny human in his arms, and just as Luci suspected, her ovaries were seconds away from combusting. This was *so* not fair.

"Hey, little man," Luci heard him whisper. "I'm your Uncle D. Someday when you're old enough, I'm gonna tell you a *lot* of stories about your old man."

Della smiled, wiping a tear from the corner of her eye.

"But only when you're old enough." Then, Luci watched as he leaned down, close to the baby's ear. "I will always be here for you, little man."

Now Luci was fighting back tears of her own.

Baby warfare was a dirty, dirty game.

After a few more agonizingly sweet moments, a nurse walked into the room.

"Okay, everyone," she said, "it's time for mama to try feeding again." Cash and Dayton took their cue, and Dayton handed Jax back to Della.

"We are going to go grab some food," Cash told her.

"No, no. You guys head home, seriously. You've been here forever. You, too, Luci," Della said.

Luci's eyes darted toward Della. There was no way she was leaving her alone. She was about to protest, when she saw Della's eyes drop down to her perfect son.

Her finger softly traced his nose, and his lips, and she kissed his forehead gently.

"We're good, really. We are going to spend the night getting to know each other. Seriously, go home. I'll need you rested up when I get back there."

Luci stood still for a moment, but as she watched, she realized that Della had all she needed. She kissed Della on the cheek, and snuggled Jax one more time before walking toward the door.

"I'll be back first thing tomorrow," she said. Della nodded. "Enjoy your first night as a mama, Mama."

Della blew her a kiss as she walked into the hall.

"Luci," Dayton said, startling her as she turned down the corridor. "I figured you'd need a ride, since I brought you here."

"Oh, yeah," she said. "I forgot."

Shit. She was exhausted. And gross. Not only was she sweating during Della's labor, but she was covered in Della's sweat, too. She needed a shower, and a bed. And time away from him. Time to soak in all she'd just witnessed, the sweetness that was her

BUMPS ALONG THE WAY

godson, the madness that was about to descend upon the Niles house.

They were completely silent as they walked out to his car, the space between them palpable after weeks of walking hand-in-hand.

"So, I know you're tired. Can we talk tomorrow?" he asked after a few minutes of silence down the road. Oh, thank God.

"Yeah. Tomorrow is fine. Just not tonight."

After a little bit longer, he parked his car in front of Della's.

"You know, you're welcome to crash at my place, if you want," he said, just as she unbuckled her seat belt.

"Thanks, but I want to start cleaning up and getting the house ready for them to come home."

"Do you need any help?" he asked.

Guilt ran through her. All he wanted was to be near her. All he wanted was to help her. All he wanted was to freaking *love* her. And shit, she wanted to do all that, too. But Seattle was waiting. The second chance at the life she'd built for herself, it was all waiting. The second chance she never thought she'd get. How could Dayton fit into that life? There was no room for him there. And if she didn't take the job, if she didn't go back to her life, and he broke her heart again, where would that leave her?

"I'm good," she said. "You should go get some rest."

He nodded, eyes dropping to his steering wheel. She opened the door, and as she moved to get out, she felt his hand wrap around her wrist.

"Luci," he whispered. She paused. "I'm not exactly sure what's happening, right now. I just hope I'm not losing you again. I can't."

Crack. Boom. Bam. Her heart burst into a

217

million tiny pieces floating around his Tahoe. She offered him a flash of a sad smile. She leaned across the armrest, and laid a long kiss on his lips.

She hoped he wasn't losing her again, either.

# TWENTY-SEVEN
*Della*

Jax had only been alive outside of her body for a few hours, now, but Della had already memorized every inch of him. She couldn't stop staring at him. The way she loved him was already overwhelming to her. The nurses had come in a few times, encouraging her to sleep while he did.

"The first twenty-four hours are a sweet spot," one nurse warned her. "Then they wake up a *lot* more. Try to sleep now."

But Della couldn't imagine doing anything but stare at his tiny face while she had the energy to do so.

The next morning, she heard the door to her room crack open as she lay with Jax asleep on her chest. Luci.

"You're back early," Della said, unsurprised by Luci's punctuality. But to her surprise, the curtain drew back, and in walked Cora.

"Oh, Cora," Della said, pulling her gown around her a little bit tighter as she tried to sit herself up without disturbing her little prince.

"I'm sorry, is now an okay time?" Cora asked. She was holding an "It's a Boy," balloon in one hand, and a bouquet of roses in another.

"It's a perfect time," Della said with the warmest smile possible, despite the throbbing pain still reverberating from her crotch.

"Oh, my gosh," Cora whispered as she took a few steps closer to the bed. Her eyes grew wide with wonder as she stared down at him. "He's so tiny," she said, and if Della wasn't mistaken, Cora's eyes had some glassiness to them.

"It's so nice of you to come see us," Della said, motioning to the chair next to her bed.

"Oh, of course," Cora said. "I had asked Luci to let me know when he was here."

"Do you want to hold him?" Della asked, and a huge smile spread over Cora's lips.

"I'd love to," she answered, hopping up to visit the sanitizer dispenser on the wall. She lifted Jax so carefully from Della's arms, then sank down slowly into the chair, staring down at him as he slept. She wiggled her finger into his, and he clutched his tiny ones around hers.

Then she sniffled, and Della knew she was crying.

"Oh, Cora," she whispered. Cora looked up at her.

"I'm sorry," she said. "I can't believe this is making me so emotional. But it is. I'm just so happy he's here, and he's fine, and you're fine."

Della wanted to reach out and hug her.

"We're good, Cora. I promise," she assured her. "We're more than good."

Cora smiled.

"So, I wanted to let you know that my parents

and I, we opened a trust fund for Jax. It will be available to him when he turns eighteen."

Della's jaw dropped, her eyes as big as saucers.

"Cora," she said, "that is so, so kind of you. But you don't need to do that." Cora smiled.

"Della, if you only knew how badly I wish I could repay you and your family. How much it weighs on me that this little boy won't have his. . . won't have his dad," she said, pausing to collect herself. "And my parents, they wanted me to let you know that they are eternally in your debt. And that if you're comfortable with it, they'd like to come meet you in a few weeks."

"That would be lovely," Della said. "We'd love to meet them." She smiled for a moment, reaching for Cora's free hand.

She understood now, just how terrifying that night must have been for Cora's parents. How terrifying and helpless they probably felt when she recounted the details of it. How their very reason for existing could have been taken in the flash of a gunshot.

She understood now, because their reason for existing was holding hers.

◊

Della was laying on a beach, the same beach she remembered from her favorite dream. The sun was rising over the horizon, bright and blinding as it popped off the white sand. She shielded her hand from it as he appeared at the cusp of the dune, his dark skin glowing in the light.

He turned in slow motion, his eyes finding her in an instant, his dazzling smile making her weak.

"Hi, baby," he said, his voice echoing. She pushed herself up onto her elbows, staring in disbelief that this cocoa god really belonged to her. Just as she opened her mouth to say hello in return, a piercing scream came from down the beach. She and Jackson whipped their heads around, trying to find the source.

It was the most deafening, shrill sound she'd ever heard. And the louder it got, the faster Jackson faded away. When she turned her head again, he was completely gone.

Out of nowhere, Luci appeared next to her on the beach. No, not on the beach. In her bedroom.

"Wake up, Mama," she whispered, nudging Della awake. "He needs boob."

Della pulled herself up in her bed, propping the pillows behind her. She stretched as she yawned and looked at the alarm clock. She'd only been asleep for forty-two minutes, and scarily enough, it was the longest stretch she'd had since they got home from the hospital.

She slipped her oversized t-shirt off over her head, letting it land on the ground next to them. Luci didn't even flinch at the sight of Della's boobs anymore; since they'd been back from the hospital, she'd seen them countless times a day. Luci knelt down to pick up the u-shaped nursing pillow, and stuck it underneath Jax. Della resituated him in her arms and laid her head back, smiling as he latched like a pro.

Luci yawned and collapsed onto the foot of the bed. Della had to admit, she and Luci were crushing this co-parenting thing they had going on.

They'd been alternating each night; Luci only woke Della for feedings, then took Jax back into her room.

As Della settled herself against her headboard, she gently patted her own cheeks, trying to zap some life back into herself. She had never been this exhausted in her entire life.

Throughout her pregnancy, countless people

had casually mentioned the whole never-sleeping-again thing.

"Enjoy sleep now," they'd say in passing at the grocery store, and she'd smile and say, "oh, I am." But little did she know that until you've actually been sleep-deprived, there was no comprehending what it felt like. Like her entire body was slowly shutting down, failing from the inside out. She thought she may actually die of exhaustion. But every time she laid eyes on Jax, she was shocked at how quickly some sort of strength rekindled itself inside of her to give him whatever he needed. Breast milk, a song, a cuddle, arms to lay in. Whatever he needed, somehow, she made sure he got it. It was like some sort of sixth sense, some sort of super mom-strength.

She couldn't describe the feeling she got every time she looked at Jax. It was the the most foreign, yet most familiar type of love she'd ever felt. She'd never known a love like it, not even with Jackson. And for the first time since she'd lost him, she felt the gaping hole in her heart fill, at least partially.

As Jax finished up and Luci began to snore, Della laid a kiss on Jax's cheek before laying him down in the tiny bassinet next to her bed, then curled up in a ball and drifted back off to sleep.

Fifty-two minutes later, Della shot up from her broken sleep, panting. But all was silent. Jax slept quietly in his bassinet, and Luci still snored on her bed. It wasn't a Jackson dream, it wasn't the cries of her son. It was a burning, searing pain coming from her right breast.

She reached her fingers around her boob in the dark, letting her fingers explore it until she found the source: a *massive* lump just in front of her armpit. She slipped off the bed and into the bathroom, careful to hop over the pile of clothes on her floor so as not to trip and make too much noise.

She flicked the light on in the bathroom, squinting as she stared in the mirror. She slipped her shirt off, examining herself. She pressed lightly on the lump, and covered her mouth as she let out a quiet yelp. Holy shit. She grabbed her cell phone, consulting the internet doctors.

A-ha. A clogged duct. She tried to remember the last time Jax had eaten off of the right side, but she was so tired, she couldn't remember. Jesus, it may have been a while.

She tried once more to massage the lump, but it won again, this time making her cry out loud in pain. Moments later, Luci appeared in the doorway.

"What's going on?" she asked, rubbing her eyes. The pain was so bad, Della had tears pooling in hers. "Dell? What is it?"

"I think I have a clogged milk duct," Della said, hunched over the sink, "and it hurts like a bitch."

"Oh, shit," Luci said, closing the toilet lid to sit on top of it as she grabbed Della's phone off the counter and began investigating. "Okay, this says warm compress. Turn on the hot water."

Della did as she was told, whimpering like a damn puppy as she let the water run. Luci handed her a towel from the rack and she ran it under the scorching water, then clutched it to her breast. After a few minutes, she removed it, attempting once more to massage it. The damn thing wouldn't budge, and now the tears were streaming down her cheeks.

For fuck's sake. As if the bottom half of her body wasn't obliterated enough, now the top half had to reciprocate?

"Okay, okay. This says massage," Luci said, looking at Della with fearful eyes.

"No fucking way. It doesn't help and it hurts like a motherfucker."

"Okay. Um. . . this says a hot shower may help," Luci said, standing up and turning on the water. Della undressed hastily, jumping into the shower. She stood for a few minutes, letting the scalding water hit her skin and praying to the milk gods for a nice flow. Yet, nothing.

Luci handed her a towel as she kept scrolling.

"This says. . . ew."

"What?" Della asked, wrapping the towel around her, careful not to pull it too tight around her breast.

"'For a stubborn duct, it may help to have your partner suck it out, as he or she will have more power than your baby.' Okay, look, being that I am your partner right now, I'm gonna have to pass on that. Sorry," Luci said. "A-ha! I think I got it!"

With that, Luci ran from the bathroom, and in a moment, returned with a sleeping Jax in her arms.

"What are you doing?" Della whispered.

"Dream feeding! Take the towel down," Luci said.

"But he's asleep," Della whispered.

"Take it *down!*" Luci said. Della sighed, doing what she was told. Luci took a step forward, positioning Jax directly in front of Della's breast. And like a hound dog on a case, he instinctively turned his head, opened his mouth, and latched on.

He sucked once, twice, three times, then scrunched his tiny face up into a bewildered look before unlatching. As soon as he came off, a stream of milk sprayed from Della's boob at what seemed to be fifty miles per hour, drenching Jax's face and the wall behind him.

Della looked up at Luci, then fell to the toilet

seat, laughing and crying at the same time. *Finally.* Her poor boob. In an instant, Jax was back to sleep.

# TWENTY-EIGHT
*Luci*

It had been almost a full month since Jax had come home from the hospital, and Luci had to admit, she was happy to be getting back to work. The time off had been nice, and as exhausting as it was, she loved being there for Della. And she *loved* taking care of Jax. But she was itching for some routine in her life again. And she wouldn't mind an adult conversation or two. She needed to see something other than the ten mustardy-shit newborn diapers a day. God, those were so freaking gross.

Dayton had been a weekly staple at the house, bringing by meals and helping Cash with odds and ends around the house, yet things between Luci and him were still off.

They hadn't been alone since the night Della went into labor, and it wasn't because Luci didn't *want* to. Every time she saw him, a swarm of butterflies swirled in her gut. Each time he smiled, even if it wasn't at her, she wanted to grab him and throw him against the wall. When he was helping her rearrange the furniture in her room the week before, and she watched every muscle in his body flex as he easily moved it around, it was all she could do not to strip him naked. But she wasn't sure what it would mean. She wanted him *so* much, in more ways than one. She wanted his body—his hot, hard, naked body—but she wanted so much more than that. She wanted him fully; she wanted him to be her first hello every morning and her last goodnight before she went to bed.

But it would mean staying in Dalesville. In some ways, it would always be home to her. But it would also mean that she'd have to trust that Jackson wouldn't leave her again. She'd have to believe they were stronger this time. She'd have to count on the idea that the shitstorm of media attention after Dayton's father was captured wasn't going to rip them apart.

Luci had sworn to Dayton that the distance between the two of them was only because she wanted to be fully present for Della. But in all honesty, she was glad she had Della and Jax to put the blame on. The truth was, she wasn't ready to face Dayton, and the decision she'd be making soon. He'd asked to see her at his place that night, and she was dreading it. Because she'd probably have to break his heart in one way or another, and in turn break her own again.

As soon as her laptop booted up at the Music Cafe, it *dinged* with the sound of an incoming message. And when she saw it was from Mia, her heart did a leap, then sank faster than the damn Titanic.

> *Luci,*
> *I wanted to let you know that the position is now open. There's still time. Let me know if I should put in a good word.*
> *Mia*

She sighed, then closed her computer as quickly as she'd opened it.

As she trudged up Della's porch steps, Luci looked up at the tiny bungalow. It was so perfect for Della and Jax. Big enough for them to each have their own space once Jax grew, yet small enough for them to never feel alone. It was their perfect home. But it just wasn't Luci's.

As she walked into the kitchen, Della lifted her head from the recliner, a sleeping Jax sprawled out on Cash's chest next to her on the couch.

"Hey," she called.

"Hey," Luci answered, trying to put a little more pep in her tone than she was actually feeling. Within moments, Della appeared in the doorway.

"What's up?" she asked.

"Oh, nothing."

"You were barely gone for an hour. Couldn't have possibly gotten much work done," Della said, pulling out one of the kitchen chairs.

Luci smiled and shrugged, reaching into the fridge for a bottle of water.

"Alright. What's going on?" Della insisted. She used her foot to nudge one of the other chairs out, eyeing it for Luci to sit down.

Luci couldn't help but smile. There was truly no hiding anything from Della.

"Well," she said, sinking down into the chair. "Mia emailed me today."

"Your boss?"

"Yep."

"And?" Della asked.

"There's a position open at one of her friend's companies, another executive position. She knows the hiring manager. She asked me if I wanted her to put in a good word," Luci said, swallowing nervously. She'd avoided bringing up anything related to her work since Jax was born until now. She didn't want to spook Della; she was determined not to cause Della an ounce of anxiety over her potential abandonment. But she needed to get this out.

"Oh, wow, Luci," Della said in a hushed tone, leaning over the table. "That's amazing. So do you want it?"

Luci looked up at her, searching for the fear, the terror at the idea of being left alone. But there didn't seem to be a hint of it at all. Luci nodded.

"Yeah, I think I do," she whispered. Della smiled, reaching out and taking her hand.

"Then you know just what to do. You email Mia back right now and tell her," Della said.

Luci looked at her again, with big, sad eyes.

"Dell, I can't leave you guys," she said. Della smiled.

"Luci, I love you for how dedicated you are to me and that little boy. But you need to remember something," she said, sitting up straighter in her chair. "This house, this life, and that baby in there, that's the life *I* chose. That's the life *I* always wanted. And you've been a freaking Godsend. But Luce, you have to live your own life. Me and him, we're gonna be okay. In case you haven't noticed, I sorta rock at this whole mommin' thing."

Della smiled as she leaned back in her chair, and Luci smiled, too.

It was true. Despite the tears, and hormones, and sleepless nights, and the fact that Della forgot to shower for the first three days she was home from the hospital, Luci was totally blown away at how naturally Della had taken to mothering. She could read Jax's needs like a book, deciphering his different cries and noises to figure out exactly what he wanted.

"Luci," Della said, leaning forward again, "I will never, *ever* be able to repay you for all you've done for us since Jackson died. You will never understand how lost I'd be without you. But it's time for you to figure out what the rest of your life is going to look like. And it's time for me and Jax to figure this thing out on our own."

Luci nodded, surprised at the tears running down her own cheeks. She knew Della was right. The time had come.

"I do have one question," Della said, wiping a tear from Luci's cheek. "Where does this leave you and Dayton?"

Luci straightened herself out, leaning back against her chair and putting a hand to her head.

"I'm not sure. He asked to see me tonight at his place."

"Well, I think you need to tell him all of this. It could still all work out, Luci. He might surprise you."

Luci smiled, a sad, half-assed smile.

That night, she flicked shirts and dresses over her shoulder onto her bed before settling on a soft, heather-red sundress with a cardigan over it. If she was going to be a bundle of nerves and crush the love of her life, she wanted to look decent while doing it.

She pulled her black curls into a bun at the nape of her neck, and made her way downstairs.

As she made her way into the living room, she heard Della whisper.

"Hot tamale!" she called out, Jax eating away at her boob. Luci smiled as she gently brushed his silky-smooth cheek.

"God, he's perfect," she said. Della plucked him

off of her chest, pulling him up onto her shoulder to burp. "Are you sure I have to go tonight? He's the only man I need in my life," Luci said, pointing to Jax.

Della rolled her eyes.

"You're going. Go. Get out of here. Be gone. Go have sex," she said. Luci laughed as she kissed them both on their foreheads.

"You sure you're good?" she asked before stepping out onto the porch. Della rolled her eyes again.

"Yes, mom. We're good," she said with a smile. "Go."

When Luci pulled up to his house, she was surprised he wasn't waiting at the door. Every time she'd come over before, he'd been waiting in the doorway with his melt-worthy smile, like she was the most amazing package that had ever been delivered at his doorstep. As she made her way up the porch steps, she saw a handwritten note taped to the doorknob.

*Come around back.*

Weird.

She turned to go back down the steps, following the perfectly landscaped stone path around the house. As she grew closer to the back yard, everything got a little brighter. The whole yard was outlined in dim string lighting. She followed the lights around to the patio, and laid eyes on him.

He was standing in the middle of the patio in a nice jacket and a dark pair of jeans, and she closed her mouth to stop any potential drool. His hair was trimmed tight, and his gray eyes were gleaming, even in the dim light. He held two glasses of champagne, and a bouquet of flowers lay next to him on the table. She swallowed, but her heart was reacting like a pinball inside the machine.

"Hi," he said, killer smile following behind. She

swallowed again.

"Hi," she whispered.

"You look beautiful."

"You're looking pretty sharp, yourself."

"So, I'm gonna say a few things," he said, turning to put the champagne down, "but please, just let me get through them before I chicken out. Then you can say whatever you want."

She didn't say anything, just nodded slowly, her eyes as wide as saucers.

"Three years ago, I had a night like this planned. I wanted to take you out, wine and dine you, and promise myself to you for the rest of my life. And then something happened, and I felt lost. I made a stupid decision, and I hurt you, and no matter what, no matter where we end up, I'll never forgive myself for that.

But those things I felt that night, those things I wanted to say. . . I never, not for one day, stopped feeling them. I know we'll never get that time back, and I know it's all my fault. But these past few months, I realized that none of the rest matters. And that when you're back in my life, everything is just sweeter."

He reached his hand into his pocket, and Luci noticed that it was shaking. He pulled out a small, black velvet box, and she swallowed again. Now, her hands were shaking. He took a step toward her, took a breath, and knelt down on one knee. He looked down, smiling at the box.

"I saved up all my tips for two years for this," he said, opening the box to reveal the most beautiful ring she'd ever seen. It was a solitaire diamond, princess cut, and it made her heart do a little jump. "I can afford something a little fancier now, but it just felt like this thing deserved to see the light of day. It's just been sitting in my drawer, waiting for me to grow a pair and realize the monumental mistake I made," he said with a sad smile.

She covered her mouth. His eyes flicked up to hers.

"I know it's fast. I know it's only been a few months. But you know me, and I know you. And I know that I don't want to do the rest of my life without you, because you make me the version of myself I want to be.

"So, with that," he said, reaching for her hand, "Luciana Catalina Ruiz, if you will take me, I promise you'll never hurt that way again. I promise I'll be there for everything. I promise to take care of you always. And I promise you as much Spongebob mac and cheese as your heart desires. Will you marry me?"

Her hand was trembling in his. His eyes were gray pools full of hope and a little panic as he waited for her to speak. She stared down at the ring in his hand, and at her hand in his. And then she burst into tears, sinking down to her own knees in front of him.

"Luci? What is it? What's the matter?" he asked, scooting toward her and taking her into his arms. "It's too soon. I'm an idiot. I'm sorry. I just didn't want to waste any more time."

She shook her head, wiping her eyes with her thumbs and sinking back to her butt on the patio. He followed her lead.

"No, no. I mean, yeah, it's soon. But that's not it. You know me. I know you, just like you said. It's not that," she said, collecting herself. "There's this job that just opened up. Another executive position. It would be an amazing opportunity. But it's back in Seattle. And the more I've been thinking about it, the more I just want to be back there. I miss the West Coast. I miss everything about it. I mean, I like visiting home. I love being close to Della, and now Jax. And I love being close to you. But my life isn't in Dalesville."

He stared out at the land in front of them, eyes wide. He nodded.

Finally, he spoke.

"So, Seattle, huh?"

# TWENTY-NINE
*Della*

She should really be asleep right now.

Everyone and their freaking mother had told her to sleep when the baby slept. Although, she was coming to realize that was the most bullshit advice ever. The second she'd get comfortable enough to drift off into sleep, some sort of internal alarm went off inside Jax that told him his mother was comfortable, and the wailing would begin.

So instead of sleeping soundly in her bed, she was pacing the floor in her foyer.

"Dude, calm down," Cash said, his eyes open wide, staring ahead as his fingers clicked around on his game controller. "They will be here."

"Well, what's taking them so long? I mean, Jesus, how long does a damn proposal take?"

Of *course* she knew about it. How else would she have known to get Luci a gift certificate for a manicure to thank her for all her help just days before?

And how else would Dayton have gotten Mr. Ruiz's number back in Cuba to ask for his permission?

But earlier that day, after the somewhat-haunting conversation Della had with Luci about the future of her and Dayton, Della had called him.

"Fair warning, I'm not really sure where her head is at. She's definitely worried about committing to stay around here."

"Well," Dayton had said, "if I learned anything the last time, it's that I'm never making that same mistake again."

"What mistake?" Della asked him.

"Not proposing. If she says no, at least I know that I didn't just let her slip through my fingers again."

Della had to hand it to him, he didn't give up easily. He was going to fight for her best friend, and it was so damn romantic. But her heart was twisted. Della wanted the sappy, beautiful love story of Dayton and Luci to play out. But more than anything, she wanted Luci to just be happy, regardless of where that left Dayton.

Finally, she heard the car pull up out front.

She ran to the kitchen, pretending to be searching the pantry for a snack so as not to give away the fact that she knew all the happenings, or, the *intended* happenings of the evening.

She heard Luci's key in the door and made her way to the foyer casually.

Luci stood in the doorway, Dayton close behind her. They both wore serious expressions, and Della couldn't miss the tears welling in Luci's eyes.

Oh, damn. This was it. This was the end of the beautiful little love story that was Luci and Dayton. She'd broken his heart.

Or, maybe he'd broken hers again. Maybe he'd chickened out after all. God *damn* it. If he did, she swore she'd castrate him right then and there. Not this time, motherfucker.

Just as her eyes were widening, Luci stuck her hand out, a bright and shiny diamond shimmering under the light of the chandelier.

"Will you be my matron of honor?" Luci asked, her hand shaking.

Della looked from the ring, to Luci, to Dayton, then back to the ring. She squealed, pulling them both into her as they spun in circles, Della bawling like a baby.

"Oh, my God!" she cried, finally gathering herself as Dayton laughed. She grabbed Luci's face, kissing her cheeks, then grabbed Dayton's and did the same. "So, what does this mean?"

"Well," Dayton said, wrapping his arm around Luci's neck and pulling her into him for a kiss, "it turns out that they *do* have a police force in Seattle," he said with a sly smile. "I'll be applying later this week, and moving there soon with my fiancée."

Della would forever remember the smile that spread across Luci's face in that moment. It was full of pure glee, an unwavering love for the man in front of her, and even a tiny bit of the heartache she'd dealt with in the past. But it was all rolled up into that beautiful smile, that showed just how much she wanted Dayton, how much the pain and the years apart were worth having him by her side now.

"But we did make a decision on the way here," Luci said, "that we want to get married here in Dalesville. So it looks like we will be making a lot of trips back here over the next year."

Now, a smile spread across Della's face. Because as elated as she was for Luci, a small part of her was terrified at the solidity of it all. It was set in stone now; Luci was leaving, and before she knew it, Cash would be gone, too. And it would just be Della and Jax. She smiled, wiping the last tear from her cheek.

"Well," she said, clapping her hands together, "it's time to plan a damn wedding!"

The next morning, Della made her way down the stairs, Jax nestled close to her chest in his carrier, snoozing away. As she walked toward the fridge, she heard Luci on a call out on the patio.

She stepped outside a few moments later with a mug of coffee in either hand, held as far from her body as possible so as not to pose a possible risk for Jax.

"Thank you," Luci mouthed, still on the phone. "Oh, yes. Oh, gosh, Mia, are you serious? I barely interviewed!"

Della sank into the chair, listening intently.

Finally, Luci spoke up again.

"Oh, my God. That's *amazing!* Yep, that timeline works perfectly. That gives my fiancé and I just enough time to find a new apartment and get settled. Yep, sounds good. Thank you so much, Mia. I owe you huge."

"Well?" Della asked, scooting to the edge of her chair.

"I talked to the hiring manager for all of ten minutes this morning, but I guess Mia gave such a rave review that he told her he was going to offer me the job! I can't believe it! They want me to start in a month."

Della clapped her hands quietly, trying to keep the movements to a minimum so she didn't disturb the sleeping prince.

"Oh, my God, Luce! I'm just so excited for you!" she cried. Luci hugged her, holding her arms wide to fit around both of them.

"I'm going to miss you guys so much," Luci whispered before pulling away.

"Ah, ah," Della said, holding up a finger. "No

making this sad. This is *everything* you deserve, Luci. Please, let yourself be happy."

# Winter, One Month Later

# THIRTY

*Luci*

She stared at the woman in front of her for a long moment, admiring her figure, the way the lace hugged her in all the right spots, the gleam of the diamond on her left ring finger. She couldn't remember the last time she felt this beautiful.

That's a lie.

She could.

It was just that morning, in bed with Dayton. She opened her eyes and rolled toward him. But he was already there, facing her, eyes squinted, scanning her every feature. It wasn't in a lustful way—they'd taken care of that the night before—but it was in complete adoration. Like he still couldn't believe she said yes, like he still couldn't believe that she came back to him.

Now, she stood on a stool in front of a flood of endless mirrors, and endless tears from her mother. Della sat nearby on a red velvet couch in the bridal shop, nursing a *very* hungry Jax.

"Damn, you're good-looking," she said, staring up at Luci.

Luci laughed and shook her head, looking back at her through the mirror. Her mother sniffled again, wiping the dripping mascara from her eyes.

"Oh, Ma," Luci said, "if you're this bad at my fitting, how bad will you be on the day of the actual wedding?"

"We're going to need to put a box of tissues at every row," her mother said, blotting away at her face.

One of the shop owners was behind Luci now, starting to undo the hundreds of perfect satin buttons at the back of the gown. Luci caught one last glimpse of herself in the dress before the woman finished freeing her from it.

It was strapless, off-white, with lace everywhere. The train was long, but not *too* long, and a long beaded sash tied around her waistline. This was only her second trip to the boutique, but she'd found the gown on a rack during their first trip, and she knew instantly that it was hers. She'd gotten her measurements done that day, and planned for her mother to keep it until the wedding.

"I'm going to go put the last payment down," her mother said, walking toward the front of the store.

"I can't believe the wedding is a year from today," Della said, pulling her shirt back down and burping Jax, who now looked completely satisfied.

"Me, either!" Luci said. One year from today, she would be a married woman. And she smiled at the huge, crazy, circular path her life had taken. Right back to Dalesville. Right back to Dayton. And soon, she'd have him with her in her city. She'd be making moves, making her father proud. She'd have everything she could have ever even dreamed of wanting.

Well, almost everything.

She turned and looked at Della again, so effortlessly caring for Jax. Just like Luci knew she would. And Jax, with his soft, mocha-skin and his perfect black curls, had wiggled his way into Luci's heart from the second she first laid eyes on him, despite all the other gross shit going on around him in that moment.

Within the week, she'd be leaving him. She'd be leaving both of them. She stepped off of the stool and swooped down to pick him up. She held him high in the air, then brought him down to her face to rub his nose.

"Be careful, Auntie Luce, or you're gonna get a face full of boob-milk puke," Della warned. Luci laughed.

"He's still little enough that his puke is cute," Luci said. She paused for a moment, settling him comfortably in her arms. "He's going to look so different the next time I see him," she said quietly, staring down at him. She felt Della's arm drape around her shoulder.

"Yeah, he is. But we have these things now, called phones," she said, waving hers in the air with a sarcastic smile on her face. "And, see, you just press this button, and, oop! There's my face. Would ya look at that?"

Luci rolled her eyes at Della, flashing her a sheepish smile.

"You know what I mean," Luci said, looking back down at her perfect little prince, now milk-drunk and passed out in her arms.

"Luci," Della said, her tone growing more serious, "don't take this the wrong way, okay? But I feel like I need this time alone as much as you need to get back to Seattle. You can't stay with me forever. I mean, I wish you could. We could be like the *Golden Girls,* except that we'd be in our twenties." Luci smiled. "But seriously. I can't get too used to you being around, or I'll become too dependent on you. Eventually, Jax and I have to figure out what our life looks like together. On our own. Me and him, against the world."

Luci nodded, swallowing back the lump growing in her throat.

"Dell, can I ask you something?"

"Yeah?"

"Are you and Jax gonna be okay, ya know, financially? I hate bringing this up, but I just want to let you know that if you need anything, we can help you out. Seriously," Luci said, squeezing Della's hand as she spoke. She'd been so worried about this for so long, but had no idea how to bring it up. No clue what to say. Not sure exactly how to ask her best friend if she was broke.

Della smiled.

"Yeah, Luce. We're gonna be okay," she said. Luci looked down at her hands. *How?*

"Jackson's company offered an amazing life insurance policy. The house is totally paid off," Della went on. "And we still have money left over. It won't last us forever, but it's enough for a while. Just enough time for me to get back to work."

Luci looked up at her, and Della smiled.

"Yep. I decided I want to get certified to be a school counselor. I just feel like there's so many of these kids who desperately need to talk. And I could be that person to listen. Since I already have my teaching degree, I just need a certification. I also already talked to your mom. . . and she's going to nanny for me," Della said, a wide grin on her face. Luci felt the tears pricking at her eyes as a wave of peace fell over her.

This was the last piece. Della and Jax, and what she thought was such an uncertain future. She'd thought it was going to be shaky and unpredictable. But she forgot she was talking about her Della.

"You two are going to be fine," she finally

managed to say, just as Della wrapped her arms around her, still holding Jax in the crook of her arm. "I'm so proud of you, Della."

As Luci walked up the steps of Dayton's little farmhouse that evening, she stopped to look out over the land, another perfect Dalesville sunset landing on the fields in front of her. The FOR SALE sign swung in the breeze, and she smiled.

Della was going to be okay. She was going to be more than okay. She was ready. And so was Luci.

She had lost time to make up for with Dayton. And she couldn't wait to get started.

# Summer, One-and-a-half Years Later

# THIRTY-ONE
*Della*

One thing about farms is that they make a heck of a wedding venue. And in Dalesville, there was no shortage of them.

The Calways had a son that graduated a year ahead of Della and Luci, and he played on the football team with Jackson and Dayton. He was more than happy to cut Luci and Dayton a deal at the family farm, and the setup was perfect.

The sun was setting perfectly just behind the altar, and Della looked around at all the guests that sat on either side of the aisle, friends from high school, Dayton's mother, Mrs. Ruiz. Even some of Luci's coworkers made the trek from Seattle, to what Della could tell they thought was the end of the earth.

Finally, soft music began to play, and everyone in the audience turned to the top of the aisle like a group of trained monkeys. Della took a few steps forward, reaching out to grab Dayton's sleeve. He smiled, squeezing her hand and winking at her.

He looked so dapper in his gray suit, his hair cut nice and neat, the nerves practically flying from his collar. She turned to the end of the aisle, where Cash sat, knelt to the ground, holding on to a wiggling, writhing Jax dressed in a miniature version of Dayton's suit. Della nodded to Cash, who took a big breath, closed his eyes, and let go.

Jax took off like a drunken horse at the gates of the Kentucky Derby, running in a zig-zag line down the aisle. He stopped to pick at a bow tied to one of the chairs, then knelt down to pick a dandelion.

He'd only been walking for about a month, so he still resembled a drunk driver attempting to pass a sobriety test.

"Jax," Della called, whispering at first. "*Jax,*" she said, a little more sternly this time.

"Come on, Jax, this way, sweetie," Aunt Bea called, now standing up from her chair.

"Go on, Jax, go to Mama," Cash called. The rest of the crowd began to stir, but everyone smiled, some giggling out loud. A hundred "awws" filled the air as Della tried to keep her cool.

She was totally content with Jax wearing the suit, but not actually participating in the ceremony. He could take a few cute pictures, be there for part of the reception. But *no.* Luci had insisted that he be an official ringbearer, despite the fact that he wouldn't actually be carrying the rings.

"It'll be adorable," Luci had said. "Some weddings are so serious. So stuffy. This will be good comic relief." At this moment, Della wanted to let Luci know that she could take her comic relief and shove it up her ass.

Suddenly, Jax froze, his attention leaving the grass, and settling on the fact that he was surrounded by a huge crowd of strange faces. This was her chance.

She could pounce during his moment of weakness. In the most loving, motherly way possible, of course.

"Jax, come to Mama," she said, holding out her arms. Finally, he picked up speed, running right to her. Cash stood at the end of the aisle now, waiting for the interception. Della passed Jax off carefully and took her place at the top of the altar once again.

The music picked up, and heads turned again. And there, at the head of the aisle, came Luci on her mother's arm. Her hair was twisted back into a perfect bun, baby's breath braided all through it. At the back of the aisle, one of Luci's cousins stood holding a phone up, Mr. Ruiz watching from Cuba.

Instantly, the tears pricked Della's eyes, but she swallowed hard, refusing to let them fall. Her makeup was expensive, and she still had pictures to take.

But damn, did her best friend look gorgeous. She watched as Luci made her way down the aisle, never for a second taking her eyes off of Dayton.

Yeah, this was love.

This was Jackson and Della kind of love.

Della smiled through the whole ceremony, wiping happy tears the whole damn time. And she loved the reaction they were waiting for when the pastor announced them "Mr. and Mrs. Ruiz," instead of Mr. and Mrs. Briggs. There were hundreds of wide-eyes, and even a few gasps.

After Dayton's father was apprehended and charged with murder, he wasn't exactly desperate to keep his name. And with Luci's corporate success, it made sense for her to keep hers.

Her last name gave him a fresh start, a breath of fresh air, untainted by his father. Della thought it was so beautiful, how all the pieces of Luci and Dayton fit together.

At the reception, Aunt Bea held Jax at the back of the tent as Della took the microphone at the front.

"Hi, everyone," she said, clearing her throat as she unfolded the piece of paper she had tucked between her boobs earlier that night. "For those of you I don't know, of which there are very few, I'm Della, Luci's best friend. We've been glued to each other's hips for over twenty years now, and though we are here tonight to celebrate the love she has with Dayton, I have something to confess: she's my soulmate."

She paused as giggles filled the room.

"Luci has been right there next to me through every single one of life's curveballs. Through every sharp turn, every bump along the way, Luci has been there to take the wheel and point me back in the right direction. She's tough, she's strong, and she loves fiercely. Which brings me to you, Dayton. This woman," she paused, gathering herself as she held a hand out to Luci, "is the definition of loyal. Just know that she will stand by your side through it all, the good, the bad, the heavy, the light."

Dayton pulled Luci in close, kissing her forehead as he nodded to Della.

"I've watched the two of you for years now," she continued, "and I know love when I see it. Take in every second, live in every single moment. Slow down, and enjoy the nights you spend on the couch as much as the ones you spend at fancy restaurants and on nice vacations. I can't wait to see the life that you two make with each other, because a life built from love is the best kind. To Dayton and Luci!"

"To Dayton and Luci!" the crowd called back, raising their glasses in the air. Dayton and Luci both stood, wrapping Della in a long embrace.

After the rest of the speeches—which, not that Della was keeping track—definitely didn't make the audience tear up as much as Della's had, the DJ started playing music, and the dance floor grew busy.

Della took the opportunity to sit at one of the back tables, slipping off her heels and leaning back against the cool metal of the chair.

She watched as Cash swirled Sharelle around, spinning her into him and holding her close. It had been six months since Cash moved out of Della's, and into his new apartment with Sharelle in Baltimore. She was quiet, but sweet as pie, and she loved him.

"They are so cute together," Cora said, plopping down in the seat next to her, slipping her shoes off, too.

"They are," Della agreed.

"I can't believe we start school in just a few weeks!" Cora said, reaching her hands back to primp her perfect locks. Della smiled.

"I know. Summer went fast, as always. But we're gonna have a blast. Your classroom is really close to the counseling office," Della said.

A counseling position had opened up at a high school a few miles outside of town, and Della had been able to snag it quickly, thanks to her teaching background.

And when she learned the school also needed a tenth-grade history teacher, Della put in a good word for Cora, and she was hired within a few weeks.

Della couldn't explain it, but in a short time, she and Cora had grown close. She felt protective over her, like Cora needed her guidance. But there was also a part of Della that needed Cora around. She wasn't exactly sure why; it may have had to do with the fact that Cora was the last one to see her husband alive. Or maybe it was the fact that Jackson died saving her.

Della felt like she had to be there for Cora; she wanted to make sure Jackson didn't die in vain. Cora was given a second chance, an opportunity that Jackson didn't get. And Della wanted to be there to make sure she made the most of her life.

And on top of that, Cora had been a really good friend.

She ate dinner with Jax and Della a few times a week, and even babysat him a few times while Della ran errands. The truth was, she popped up in Della's life right when she needed her.

As Cora and Della people watched from their seats, a buff young man who was on the force with Dayton back in Dalesville made his way smoothly to their table. Della smiled; she'd seen him making eyes at Cora all night long. He cleared his throat a few times before speaking.

"H-hi," he said, "I'm Bobby. Would you maybe want to dance?"

Cora smiled bashfully before taking his hand.

"Oh, yes, I would," she answered, her voice shaky and her cheeks flushed. "I'm Cora, by the way."

"Hi, Cora," Bobby said with a smile.

"Be right back," she whispered to Della as she stood up. Della smiled.

"Take your time."

Della watched as one of Luci's uncles danced stiffly with Aunt Bea as she talked his ear off. Then Della sat at attention. Aunt Bea was supposed to be watching Jax.

Where the fuck was he? Why would she leave him? Just as she sprung to her feet, she looked to the center of the dance floor. Dayton swayed back and forth, one arm snug around Luci's waist, the other hoisting Jax up between them. Jax giggled as Luci knelt in to touch her nose to his, her arm wrapped around the other side of him.

Della sat back down again, a sigh of relief lifting the weight from her chest. The feeling of someone she loved also loving her child was one that she came to savor. For most of Jax's short life, Luci and Dayton had lived thousands of miles away from him. But they video chatted at least twice a week, and they'd made the trip back to Dalesville every other month. They'd done an amazing job of being in his life, even if they couldn't be there physically. And it showed in how comfortable he was with them. Della's heart swelled as she flicked another damn tear out of the corner of her eye. Damn motherhood hormones.

"They make an amazing couple, don't they?" she heard a deep, silky-smooth voice ask.

"They do," she said, glancing up at him. He was tall and slim, but his defined shoulders pulled tight on his dress shirt. His short blond hair shimmered in the last of the sunlight, and his ocean-colored eyes were striking.

"I'm Cole Davis. I work with Dayton," he said, sticking out a large hand. She shook it with a quick smile.

"I'm Della. So you're a cop?" she asked.

"I am, but don't hold it against me," he said, flashing her a smile that she guessed had weakened a few knees in its day. She smiled back, holding her hand out to offer him a seat at her table.

"So, the ringbearer is yours?" he asked. She turned to admire her greatest accomplishment yet again.

"He is," she said dreamily.

"He's beautiful."

"Thank you," she said.

"His father was Jackson Niles, right?" he asked. She closed her eyes, still never quite prepared for the blow delivered to her heart every time she heard Jackson's name.

"He was."

"From what I've been told, he was a hell of a man." She smiled.

"He was."

"I'm just glad the bastard that shot him got a life sentence," Cole said. Della nodded.

"And no possibility for parole," she said, a quick but nervous smile flashing over her lips.

It had been months since the trial ended, but some days it still felt so fresh. And some nights, she woke up in a sweat, worried he was still out there, forgetting he was as good as dead in prison somewhere.

But then she'd remember the last moment she saw him, his face scrunching into a fit of ugly tears as the police escorted him from the courtroom. Tears streaming down her own face and down Cora's. Della and Dayton with their hands on her shoulders.

It was one of the biggest reliefs of her life. And even though Timothy Band still haunted her sometimes, she was getting better. She was getting through it.

"The single parenting thing is tough. My wife left my daughters and I two years ago," Cole said after a long silence.

"Oh, I'm sorry to hear that," she said, putting her hand to her chest. Although she felt for the man, she also couldn't fathom a mother leaving her children. Her eyes found Jax again, frantic at just the thought.

"I don't know about you, but I still wake up every day feeling like something's missing. Or someone. I don't know how to explain it, but it just feels like something is still a little bit. . . broken."

She heard what he was saying, and she felt like her answer should be in line with his. Lord knew how she'd struggled without Jackson. She'd missed his laughter, and the way he could make her laugh, even when she was angriest at him.

She'd missed his attitude, the nonchalant way he just took care of things. She'd missed his touch, the way he made love to her, the way he nuzzled the back of her neck after a long work day. And when Jax came along, she missed having someone to share it all with. The amazingly good, and the soul-crushing bad.

But then, Della looked back at the dance floor, at her beautiful best friend dancing with her new husband. She looked at the light in Luci's eyes when she gazed up at Dayton, and the pride in his when he looked back at her. She stared at the perfect little human she created with the love of her own life, and she felt something she hadn't felt in so long: peace.

She knew a piece of her would forever be with Jackson, and whenever, *if* ever someone new were to come in, he would never hold her whole heart.

But maybe, someday, she'd find love again.

That was the thing, though: she wasn't looking for it. She already *had* it. Not in the conventional way, where she had a partner that she walked through life with.

Instead, she had a miniature version of that partner, and instead of walking through life with him, she spent hers chasing *after* him. But it was beautiful, and full, and exactly what she needed. She had it in the inexplicable, immeasurable love she had for Jax.

She had it in the love of her soulmate, Luci. And she had it in the love and pride she'd begun to feel toward herself ever since she became a mother; ever since she began putting the remaining pieces of her life back together. If she met someone down the line, it would just be the cherry on top. But if not, a sundae without a cherry is still delicious.

"Actually," she said, "I feel like everything is right where it's supposed to be. And I think we're all going to be alright."

# BUMPS ALONG THE WAY

## Acknowledgements

First and foremost, I have to thank my kiddo. Because without you and the wonderful rollercoaster ride of motherhood, this book would not exist.

To my entire family, for making motherhood so amazing by loving my kid like he's your own.

Lizzy Bee, thank you for a) your AMAZING edits, and b) for being my go-to for more than two decades.

Nyletak, thank you for standing by my side since 1996.

Sarah, thank you for being on the mama ride with me, and for all the laughs along the way as we try to figure out what the heck we're doing.

Will, thank you for being so supportive of this adventure.

SJ! Where would I be without you?! Still staring at a blank screen. That's where. #writerbesties.

And last but not least, thank you SO much to all of my amazing blogger buddies who continue to support my books and my writing career! You guys seriously make the #bookstagram world go round, and we'd all be lost without you!

**About Taylor**

Taylor Danae Colbert is a romance and women's fiction author. When she's not chasing her toddler or hanging with her husband, she's either reading a book, or writing one. Taylor lives in Maryland, where she was born and raised. For more information, visit www.taylordanaecolbert.com.

Follow Taylor on Instagram and Twitter, @taydanaewrites, and on Facebook, Author Taylor Danae Colbert, for information on upcoming books!

## Note from the Author

Dear Reader,

I can't tell you what it means that you've decided, out of all of the books in all the world, to read mine.

If you enjoyed reading it as much as I enjoyed writing it, please consider leaving an Amazon or GoodReads review (or both!). Reviews are crucial to a book's success, and I can't thank you enough for leaving one (or a few!)

Thank you for taking the time to read BUMPS ALONG THE WAY.

Always,
TDC
www.taylordanaecolbert.com
@taydanaewrites